Get ready for the festive season as
Harlequin Romance brings you a Yuletide
treat full of Christmas sparkle in this
delightful, heartwarming trilogy.

Holiday Miracles

Three sisters discover the magic of Christmas

Join sisters Faith, Hope and Grace McKinnon as they
finally come home to cozy Beckett's Run, a small
town with Christmas stockings—full of charm!

Snowbound in the Earl's Castle
Fiona Harper
October 2012

Sleigh Ride with the Rancher
Donna Alward
November 2012

Mistletoe Kisses with the Billionaire
Shirley Jump
December 2012

For Faith, Hope and Grace, this Christmas will be one
that they will *never* forget....

Dear Reader,

When Donna Alward, Fiona Harper and I all came up with the idea for three sisters from three countries coming together for a special Christmas, I remember the magic and electricity in the air while we brainstormed. We were at an outdoor café, having some fabulous food, and our brains just clicked. Within minutes, we had fleshed out the idea and found our characters.

We were thrilled that the editors at Harlequin loved the idea as much as we did, and gave us the go-ahead on the books. I always enjoy working with friends, and Donna and Fiona are some of the nicest, most generous authors on the planet. It was a great privilege to write these books with them, and to build our real-life friendship at the same time. I wish we all lived in Beckett's Run and could get together for a coffee once in a while!

I hope you love Grace, Hope and Faith as much as we did, and get wrapped up in the magical Christmas setting of Beckett's Run. Wherever you are, may your holiday be blessed by good times, good friends and good memories!

Happy reading,

Shirley

SHIRLEY JUMP

Mistletoe Kisses
with the Billionaire

HARLEQUIN®
entertain, enrich, inspire™

Recycling programs
for this product may
not exist in your area.

ISBN-13: 978-0-373-17849-0

MISTLETOE KISSES WITH THE BILLIONAIRE

First North American Publication 2012

www.Harlequin.com

Printed in U.S.A.

New York Times bestselling author **Shirley Jump** didn't have the willpower to diet, nor the talent to master under-eye concealer, so she bowed out of a career in television and opted instead for a career where she could be paid to eat at her desk—writing. At first, seeking revenge on her children for their grocery store tantrums, she sold embarrassing essays about them to anthologies. However, it wasn't enough to feed her growing addiction to writing funny. So she turned to the world of romance novels, where messes are (usually) cleaned up before The End. In the worlds Shirley gets to create and control, the children listen to their parents, the husbands always remember holidays and the housework is magically done by elves. Though she's thrilled to see her books in stores around the world, Shirley mostly writes because it gives her an excuse to avoid cleaning the toilets and helps feed her shoe habit.

To learn more, visit her website at www.shirleyjump.com.

Books by Shirley Jump

RETURN OF THE LAST MCKENNA*
HOW THE PLAYBOY GOT SERIOUS*
ONE DAY TO FIND A HUSBAND*
THE PRINCESS TEST
HOW TO LASSO A COWBOY
IF THE RED SLIPPER FITS
VEGAS PREGNANCY SURPRISE
BEST MAN SAYS I DO

*The McKenna Brothers trilogy

Other titles by this author available in ebook format.

To Donna Alward and Fiona Harper, two of the nicest writers I know. I admire your business smarts, undying kindness and giving hearts, and am proud to call you friends.

CHAPTER ONE

THE envelope sat on Grace McKinnon's hotel-room desk in Santo Domingo for a good three hours before she picked it up and glanced at the return address.

Beckett's Run, Massachusetts.

Her grandmother had to be pretty determined to track her down all the way out here. But that was Gram. When she wanted something, she got it. A stubbornness Grace had inherited—a curse, her mother called it, a blessing Gram always said. Either way, right now, Grace had bigger issues to deal with, so the envelope would have to wait.

"I just turned in the Dominican Republic piece a couple hours ago," Grace said into the phone. "Where do you want me to go next?"

The cell connection faded as she paced the room, passing the desk and the letter several times before coming to a stop again. She shifted back to the window, perched against the farthest southern pane. Below the ten floors of the hotel, cars congested the roads of Santo Domingo, impatient horns blaring an angry chorus in the bright morning sun.

Grace's hip nudged the desk and dislodged the envelope again. She leaned on the corner of the desk, toward the strongest cell signal she could find, and fingered the envelope while she listened to her boss's latest rant.

"I don't want you to go anywhere next. I skimmed what you emailed and the Dominican piece was okay, full of the usual hotspots for tourists and that kind of thing, but honestly, that New Zealand one was a mess. You kept veering off on other tangents, like the tents set up by the homeless. What tourist wants to see that? That's the kind of piece someone would write for that tearjerker *Social Issues*. Not what I hired you for and not what you said you wanted to write."

"It is what I want to write."

"Yeah? Then why do you keep sending me these change-the-world things?"

She bit back a sigh. "Wouldn't it be nice to run something different once in a while?"

"Hell, no. The advertisers don't want different. Neither do the readers. So just give me what I'm paying you for."

"I will." She shifted her weight again. In the last couple of years, all those happy vacation stories had gotten on her nerves. She wanted more. The problem was, she didn't have the chops to write more. She'd sent a few pieces to *Social Issues,* thinking she'd be a shoo-in because the editor, Steve Esler, had been her mentor in college and a good friend since then. For years he'd encouraged her to come over to the magazine and write something with "depth and meaning." She'd sent him those pieces, then sat in his office and watched him shake his head.

"You're a better writer than this, Grace. You need to put your heart into your stories. Then the reader will laugh and cry right along with you. These articles...they feel like you're afraid to care."

So she'd gone back to travel writing, to the empty kind of writing about the best hotels and zipline tours she'd written before. She told herself she was happy, that she didn't want to be one of those starry-eyed fresh-from-college journalism grads who thought they could change the world with their pen.

Except a part of her had always felt that way. And still did. Even if she wasn't a good enough writer to do that.

"I don't want humanity's woes smeared all over the page," her editor was saying. "I want happy destination recaps and most of all laughing people, who are completely unaware there is a single issue in the world worth worrying about while they sip their margaritas and enjoy a relaxing massage."

Paul Rawlins let out a long sigh. Even all the way from Manhattan, she could hear her editor's discontent.

"You let me down, Grace. Again. I can't count on you anymore."

"One mistake, Paul. The pictures—"

"It's not just one. It's many. Your stories are flat lately. Uninspired. You even made Fiji boring, for Pete's sake. *Fiji*. What happened? You used to be my best free-lancer."

"Nothing happened."

But something had. Something had shifted inside her when she'd been in Russia and seen that little girl on the streets, wearing nothing more than a thin summer dress in the middle of winter while she peddled news-papers that no one wanted to buy. Grace had taken a photo and, through a translator, gathered enough infor-mation to write a story, thinking maybe someone some-where would see it and champion the cause of homeless orphans.

But the article hadn't made it past the *Social Issues*

editor's desk because it hadn't done its job—moved the reader to act. The editor there was right. Grace McKinnon's heart was surrounded by a wall, one Grace had never been able to break. She should stick to what she knew and stop trying to be something she wasn't.

She'd get back to work, and somehow it would all work itself out. If she buried herself in work she'd be fine. Just fine.

"Why don't you take a break, Grace?" Paul said. "Just a couple weeks. Take a vacation, then come back to work."

She bristled. "Take a break? But I'm at the height of my career here."

"No. You're not."

His words, flat and final, drove the last spike into Grace's hopes.

She had lost her groove somewhere along the way. For years she'd jetted from here to there, flitting around the world like a hummingbird in a flower garden. Her career as a travel writer for one of the largest destination magazines in the world had suited her just fine. No real ties to anything or anyone, and a job that depended on one person—herself.

Then she had run into an assignment that had changed her life, changed her thinking, and everything since then had paled in comparison. She'd left the travel magazine world for the deeper pieces of *Social Issues,* and when that hadn't panned out she'd returned to travel writing, but something was wrong, an off beat, a missed step.

She kept trying to find a way back to the writer she had been before, and failing. Maybe if her sister had come when she'd called, Grace could have taken that last piece to the next level. Hope's photographic eye always saw the best in everything. But, no, Hope had refused her. Grace still smarted about that turndown. The one time she'd needed Hope—

Hope had said no.

In the last few months the magazine assignments had trickled away to almost nothing. And the last few jobs—

Well, Paul was right. They hadn't been Grace's best work. They hadn't even been her close-to-best work. Still, the thought of having all that time over the holidays stretching ahead of her with no way to fill it—

"Paul, let me do the Switzerland piece that I pitched last week. There's this train there that takes people up to the mountain. Real travel hotspot. I can cover it from the point of view of the locals—the people who live up there and need to take it down to the hospital—"

"Give it a rest, Grace. Seriously. It's almost Christmas. Just take some time off, get your wind back and call me after the holidays. We'll be needing pieces on romantic holiday destinations then. And if…" He paused. "And I mean *if* you are really ready to come back, *then* we'll talk about you going to Switzerland."

In other words, take the vacation. Or else. At least he hadn't outright fired her. The job would be there as soon as the holidays were over. She'd sit on a beach somewhere and sip margaritas and tell Paul she'd recouped like crazy. What choice did she have, really? She needed this job, and if Paul thought she needed a vacation to keep it, well, she'd do that. Or pretend. "Sure. Will do."

"Good." The relief bled through his voice, across the miles and around the world. He said goodbye, and then he was gone.

Leaving Grace alone in her hotel room, without a job or a destination. She hadn't been this adrift in…years. Maybe more than a decade.

Outside, the constant busy stream of traffic beeped

and chugged its way through Santo Domingo. She crossed to the window, watching people hurrying on their way to their jobs. Landscapers hitching rides on the back of flatbeds, hotel workers riding three to a moped, taxi drivers weaving in and out of the dense traffic jam. The salty tang of ocean air mingled with the constant fumes of congestion, giving the city a curious sweet/sour smell. All around her stood stone buildings as old as time, the foundation of North America's history, the first stepping stone for Christopher Columbus himself. Santo Domingo was a beautiful, tragic city. One she had loved. Her digital camera was full of images for her scrapbook. Not a one of them featured the beautiful beaches of Punta Cana or the bustling open air markets. No, the pictures Grace took featured other sides of the city, of the countries she visited. The kind of pictures her editor didn't want, the kind that would never accompany a story about the best vacation spots in Latin America. The kind that she had once thought would launch a career built on depth, meaning.

Why couldn't she just give up that idea? Be happy she was employed and paid to travel the world? Why did she keep searching for the very things she wasn't meant to have?

She paced around the room some more, then started packing. She loaded the last of her things into her duffle bag, then hefted it off the bed and set it by the door. Then she stood in the center of the room—

Lost.

Where was she going to go from here? The beach? Alone? At Christmas?

If anything screamed *loser,* that would be it. Sitting in some romantic destination, sipping margaritas by herself, watching all those families and couples on holiday frolic in the surf. Grace liked to be alone, but not in a place where everyone was paired off like the animals on Noah's ark.

What she needed was a destination that could serve two purposes—give her the vacation she'd promised Paul she would take, and give her an opportunity to write a bonus piece, one that really showed him she still had what it took. Sure, a little quiet time might be good, too. Give her a chance to catch up on her emails. Finally figure out that social media thing, perhaps.

But where?

Grace's attention landed on the letter from Gram. She'd almost forgotten it. She retrieved it from the desk, then tore it open, expecting the usual Christmas news and a gift card to the mall.

Instead, a plane ticket slipped out and tumbled to the floor. Grace's gaze dropped to Gram's loopy writing.

Dearest Grace,
I hope this letter finds you well. I've missed seeing you and was so disappointed when you had to cancel your trip home last year. And the year before that. I've decided that this is the year I'll see all my family for the holidays. I'm not getting any younger, and seeing you is high on my list for Santa. So, please, come home to Beckett's Run. It promises to be a wonderful holiday here, what with the town's two-hundredth-year celebration and all the festivities planned for that shindig. You wouldn't believe the event that is turning into! Something worthy of the front page, that's for sure.
I've enclosed a plane ticket. So no more excuses, sweetheart. Come home.
Love always,
Gram

Grace picked up the ticket from the floor. Go home to Beckett's Run for Christmas. To anyone else, a visit to the cozy little Massachusetts town with its snowy, magical holiday setting would sound perfect. Very Norman Rockwell-ish. But to Grace...

It sounded like torture.

Beckett's Run. The very place that contained everything—and everyone—she had run from years ago. Did she really want to revisit all that?

Then she glanced at the letter again. Two-hundred-year celebration. Big events planned. The cliché of a small town getting together for the holidays. The wheels in her head began to turn, and she made her decision. She hefted her bag onto her shoulder and headed out of the hotel.

And back to Beckett's Run.

The holiday had descended upon Beckett's Run like ten feet of snow. In a matter of days, the town had gone from winter doldrums and hues of gray and white to bright red and green, with cheery music piping from the storefronts and crimson swags swinging from light to light. The bench sitting in front of Ray's Hardware and Sundries boasted a bright red bow, the statue of town founder Andrew Beckett had a wreath necklace, and even the cement frog sitting on the front of Lucy Wilson's lawn sported a bright red Santa hat.

J. C. Carson slowed his Land Rover as he passed Carol's Diner, sending a wave in the direction of the Monday Morning Carp Club—Al, Joe and Karl, who claimed the carp was for their fishing trips, but in J.C.'s opinion it was for the observing and reporting they did from the bench in front of Carol's every day. J.C. turned right at the stop sign, then circled back around to the town park. Volunteers filled the snow-dusted space, while they worked like bundled-up bees to complete the setup for the town's holiday celebration. The first Beckett's Run Winter Festival had been planned by Andrew Beckett himself, and in the two centuries since the event had grown to include visits from Santa, sleigh-ride races down Main Street and Christmas-tree-decorating competitions. That meant the two-hundred-year-milestone celebration had a lot to live up to and a lot to outdo.

J.C. had heard one TV crew was already camped out at Victoria's Bed and Breakfast. No one was surprised—Beckett's Run had recently been voted "Most Christmas Spirit" by a world-renowned magazine, and that had the media spotlight focused on the tiny town's party.

That meant J.C. had to ensure one thing—the smooth running of the holiday event. Ten years ago no one would have pegged J.C. as the one to keep the town running on an even keel. Heck, he'd been tearing up these streets and running wild. But that had been before, and he had stopped being that J.C. a long time ago.

Beckett's Run wasn't exactly overrun with crime—a fact evidenced by the five-person police department—so J.C. didn't expect any real trouble, but planned for it just in case. The kind of publicity the article would bring would also bring in tourist dollars—something struggling Beckett's Run needed. Too many shops had been shuttered, too many houses sold. In the last couple of years J.C. had done all he could to shore up the town's waning economy, but finally realized if no one else believed in the town, there was only so much one man could do.

It was part of the reason why he'd volunteered to head up the committee for this year's celebration. He'd seen

Beckett's Run die a little more each year, after economic and personal blows hammered away at the town's core. He loved this town, and if a Christmas celebration could restore the town's faith in itself, J.C. wanted to be part of that effort. And in the process attract some much-needed tourist dollars to the coastal Massachusetts town.

But there was more, much more, he hoped the Winter Festival could do. What had started as a way to help Beckett's Run—and stop Pauline Brimmer from calling him and begging him to chair the committee—had become something personal to J.C. Something that mattered more than an economic boost to the town.

The day his life had turned upside down, J.C. had taken a leave of absence from his position at Carson Investments, given his Boston apartment key to his housekeeper, then driven out to Beckett's Run and moved back into his old room at his mother's house. He was too tall and too old for the rickety twin in his baseball-filled room, but sometimes there were more important things in life than whether his feet hung over the end of the mattress. Soon he'd have to return to Boston.

Which meant he needed to make some hard decisions. And fast.

But for now there was the Winter Festival. One challenge at a time.

J.C. turned the last corner, then released an easy breath. The downtown area all looked good. The perfect image of a serene yet festive holiday.

A sense of ownership and pride filled J.C. as he looked around Beckett's Run. When he was a kid, he'd hated this place and wanted nothing more than to leave. He'd broken the rules, come close to spending some time in the police station, even. Then he'd grown up, gone to work, and put that past behind him.

He might not have pictured himself returning to this town, but he could see why people put down roots and raised their children here. Beckett's Run offered stability, a sense of home, in its predictable schedule and dependable sameness. Something J.C.'s family needed right now. Desperately.

He heard a screech, the sharp whine of tires arguing with ice. J.C. swung the S.U.V. around just in time to see a cherry-red convertible slide past a stop sign and plow into a snowbank.

J.C. was the closest to the accident, so he pulled over and got out of the S.U.V. The cold air hit him fast and hard, whipping icy breath along his skin. He zipped his jacket, fished in his pockets for his gloves, then stepped over to the driver's side of the car.

The glass slid down, but all J.C. saw was the back of a woman's head. Long blonde hair, swept into a ponytail that swung around a thick dark blue jacket with a faux-fur-trimmed hood. "You okay, ma'am?"

"Sorry, Officer. My license is in here somewhere," she said, cursing as she rooted through the front pocket of a backpack. "Ah, finally."

She spun back, a white piece of plastic in her hand, but J.C. didn't need to look at her ID. He already knew who she was. He recognized her even with the oversize Hollywood sunglasses on her face, the bright pink lipstick on her lips, and the cherry-red convertible.

"Grace McKinnon." The words came out flat, without a single note of surprise. Though if anyone had forced him to name ten people he never expected to see in Beckett's Run again, Grace would have been in the top three.

She leaned back against the black leather seat and cupped a hand over her eyes. "J.C.?"

"The one and only."

She laughed. "Oh, my goodness. The last time I saw you...well, I can't remember the last time I saw you."

Did she truly not remember? Because he sure as hell did. Or maybe she didn't want to remember. Probably a good thing. A damned good thing. The past was behind him for a reason, and it would stay that way.

She leaned both elbows on the windowframe and shook her head. "God, I thought you were a cop. That's the last thing I need right now. I'm glad it was just you."

"Just me?"

She shrugged. "Someone who knows me."

He didn't know what to say to that. He'd once thought he knew Grace as well as he knew himself. He'd been wrong.

"And what are you doing, calling me *ma'am?*" she went on. "That makes me sound grown-up and old, and I'm neither of those."

His gaze traveled over her curves, making a quick detour down the open V of her red shirt. Damn. He begged to differ on the grown-up part. Grace had grown up and out in very nice ways.

He tried to remember why he was here. Oh, yeah. Reckless driving. Not reckless thoughts.

"You were speeding, Grace." He waved at the streets behind him. "The roads are slick, and there are a lot of people around here. I'm not a cop, but I am a concerned citizen. Do me a favor and take it easy."

She snorted. "J.C., come on, you know me. Since when do I take it easy on anything? And when did you ever want me to, at that?"

He braced a palm on the roof of her car, then leaned in until his gaze connected with those fiery hazel eyes and sent memories of the two of them together rushing through his mind. He shrugged them off. What had happened between him and Grace happened a long time ago. Hell, a lifetime ago. One where he'd been a different person, with different goals, wants and needs. "I do know you, which is why I'm asking you to take it slow."

"You sound like my father when you talk like that. What happened to the J.C. I remember?"

"He grew up." J.C. gave the roof of the car a tap, then stepped away. "Welcome back to Beckett's Run, Grace. Where life moves slower than you, remember?"

He left her sputtering and returned to his S.U.V. As he pulled away and headed down the street, Grace McKinnon gave him a very unladylike—and very Grace—glare. He was pretty sure she also shouted something he didn't want to hear.

Grace was back. And that meant Trouble had arrived in Beckett's Run.

CHAPTER TWO

GRACE pulled to a stop outside the robin's-egg-blue, Cape-Cod-style house. She hadn't been here in years, but she knew every nook and cranny of the rooms inside. Knew which board on the porch squeaked an announcement to past-curfew footsteps. Knew which way to jiggle the back doorknob when it stuck in the summer heat. Knew how many steps it took to get from her room to Faith's, and how many more to Hope's.

Of course neither of her sisters were here now, so there'd be no giggling and running down the halls. Not that they'd done much of that anyway. Serious Hope, always so worried about the younger two. Cautious Faith, the middle sister, who wouldn't have been caught dead speeding down the main thoroughfare of Beckett's Run. And then there was Grace.

That was how most folks in Beckett's Run referred to the sisters: Hope, Faith, oh, yeah, and then there was Grace. The wild one. The troublemaker.

Grace had spent nearly every summer and school break of her life in this little four-bedroom house. Her mother off on yet another vacation with yet another man, or pursuing yet another hobby she claimed would be her new career, while her three daughters spent the summer months under Gram's supervision.

Gram had gone all out on the decorations this year—as she did every year. Twin trees sat on either side of the porch, strung with white lights that swooped from balustrade to post, and all around the porch. A giant wreath filled the front door, while a candy-cane fence marched along the front walk. Blinking multicolored lights drenched every shrub, and coiled up the lamp post at the head of the driveway.

Grace got out of the car and walked around to the front. No damage from the snowbank. Thank God. The last thing she needed right now was an expensive car repair bill—on a rental, no less. J.C. had made it sound like she was committing a federal crime when all she'd done was skid a little. Okay, maybe she had been speeding. But not much. J.C. just needed to get a grip.

The last time she'd seen J.C. he'd turned away from her. Odd that they'd repeat that scenario—except without the crying and the broken heart—all these years later. He'd gotten taller, more mature, and she supposed so had she. They'd become different people, and whatever might have been between them before had surely died in the interim.

She shrugged off the thoughts of J.C. She wasn't going to be in town long, and certainly not long enough to run into him again, not that she even wanted to. He was a memory, a past she had put to rest a long time ago. Then why did she wonder what he was doing in town? How his life had turned out? If he remembered her the way she remembered him?

Before Grace could climb the stairs, Gram burst out of the house, a wiry, agile woman with a pouf of white hair and a wide smile. A reindeer-decorated apron swung around her hips as she rushed forward, arms out. "Grace! You're here!"

Grace stepped into her grandmother's embrace. A sense of warmth and home enveloped her, the same kind of steady comfort that being around her grandmother inspired. Grace may have hated Beckett's Run, with its quirky traditionalism and uninspired living, but she loved her grandmother. "Hi, Gram."

"I'm so glad you came." She drew back and smiled at Grace. Tears brimmed in her gentle blue eyes and the wrinkles on her face eased into a well-worn smile. "I've missed you so much."

"I've missed you, too." Grace shrugged her duffle higher on her shoulder and avoided the real question in Gram's eyes—why had it taken so long for Grace to return? "So...what's for dinner?"

Gram laughed and turned to lead the way into the house. "How'd I know you were going to say that?"

"The same way I know whatever you make will be fantastic." Grace pressed a hand to her belly. "And I'm famished, so I hope dinner is ready soon."

"It will be. And it'll be a great time to talk and catch up." Gram took Grace's coat and hung it in the little closet by the door, still stuffed with coats from years past—thick snowsuits, playful bright raincoats, matching gingham jackets—as if the McKinnon girls would age backward at any time. Nothing changed at Gram's—which was exactly what Grace loved about this cluttered, charming house. She dumped her duffle on the floor, then turned toward the living room.

Christmas had exploded in her grandmother's house, or at least that was what it seemed like. A thick, chubby fir tree sat in one corner, every branch lit by twinkling white bulbs or shining with an iridescent rainbow of ornaments. Gram's Santa collection marched along the fireplace mantel, up the staircase, and down the long side table in the hallway. The usual navy throw pillows had been switched for ones in festive reds and greens, and Gram's favorite pink afghan had been stowed, replaced by the reindeer one Aunt Betty had knit for her at least twenty years ago. Electric candles centered the windows, and bright red bows hung from the corners of the curtains.

Grace paused when her gaze landed on the fireplace. "You put out the stockings."

"Do you want me to take your bag up to your room?" Gram asked.

"Gram, why are the stockings out?"

"Because it's Christmas. I fixed up your old room. Clean sheets on the bed and a nice thick down comforter. You've been globetrotting so much you might have forgotten how cold these New England winter nights can get. If you need an extra blanket, look in the closet. There's—"

"Gram, you only put out the stockings for people who are going to be here on Christmas Day." Grace turned back to her grandmother. "Why did you hang up Hope's, Faith's and mine?"

Gram shrugged. Avoided Grace's gaze. "I was thinking we'd have a nice, traditional family holiday."

Nice and *traditional* meant sitting down at the table, all of them together, just like when they'd been children. Pretending they were happy, that their world was a rosy, perfect place. Grace had long ago given up on such fantasies, and had no desire to feign happiness with either of her sisters. Especially since she wasn't talking to one of them and the other was on the opposite side of the world. "Are Hope and Faith here? In town?"

"No." Gram turned away and busied herself with putting on a pot of coffee. "Not exactly."

"What's that mean?"

"I invited them for the holidays, too."

Grace bit back a sigh. Her grandmother was always doing things like this. Thinking if she just got the three McKinnon sisters together, they'd bond like glue. Turn into a happy family right before her eyes. The chances of that happening were so slim no sane oddsmaker would place a bet. And after the argument she'd had with Hope…

Well, those odds became darn near anorexic.

"I can't stay long," Grace said, already itching to be back in the convertible and heading for the closest airport. If she left soon enough she'd miss the holiday rush of travelers. And miss her sisters. That would be one way to ensure a happy, stress free holiday. "Just popping in for a couple days."

Gram's light blue gaze met hers. "Why? Do you have an assignment to get off to?"

Grace wanted to lie, she really did, but she'd never been able to lie to Gram. She loved her grandmother too much to do that, and respected the woman who had been instrumental in Grace becoming the person she was. "No. I don't. Not for a while."

An indefinite while.

"Good." Gram grinned and clapped her hands. "Because I have a favor to ask you."

J.C. strode into the Steaming Mug Coffee Shop shortly after ten on Tuesday morning and greeted the girl behind the counter. "How you doing, Macy?"

"Just fine, Mr. Carson." She grinned, revealing the same gap in her front teeth that marked her as Ron's daughter. J.C. had known Ron almost as long as he'd known his own name, and had watched Macy grow from a fussy baby to a perky, cheerful high school senior. Damn, the time passed fast. Every time J.C. saw Macy he thought of how his own life path had detoured away from a family.

"That's good to hear."

"Oh, I've been meaning to tell you," Macy said. "You were right. That Comparative Societies class was amazing. I love the professor."

"I'm glad you're enjoying it. I remember taking Professor Smith's class. He made even the most boring topics interesting."

Macy nodded. "He's wicked smart. I just love that school. I can't thank you enough for helping me out. I never could have afforded it on my own. It's just so cool that I can finally do what I dreamed of doing."

He waved off the thanks. "It was nothing, really. I just knew you deserved a good education."

"It was a lot to me," Macy said quietly.

J.C. just nodded, uncomfortable with the praise. He'd paid for Macy's education to help a friend, nothing more.

A part of him envied her the chance to go after her degree in Graphic Design. As long as he'd known Macy she'd been doodling something or other. He remembered when he'd been her age and thought he could make a career out of music. A foolish moment, J.C. reminded himself, and far in the past.

Macy brightened and grabbed a coffee mug from the tower of them beside her. "The usual?"

"Oh, yeah, sure. Thanks." He waited by the counter, drumming his fingers on the oak surface, while Macy poured a mug of the café's special dark brew. She slid the mug across the counter, and waved off—for the thousandth time—J.C.'s attempt to pay.

"My dad would have a cow if I ever let you pay," Macy said.

He stuffed the bills into a squat clear jar on the counter, emblazoned with the image of a local resident raising money for a children's charity. Macy gave him a knowing smile, then went back to work.

J.C. turned around, his gaze roaming over the small shop, looking for a free table. He picked up a copy of that day's paper from the rack by the register, sliding the thirty-five cents across the counter to Macy. If he was lucky, he'd have enough time to finish his coffee and a few headlines before he had to get to the meeting for the Beckett's Run Winter Festival. His to-do list was long, and the stress of all that—coupled with a family who seemed to need him more every day—weighed on J.C.'s shoulders.

A burst of laughter came from the couches at the back of the room. J.C. smiled. The Tuesday morning book club. A nice bunch of older ladies, who made their opinions about the literary classics well known. They'd been here every week for as long as he could remember.

That was life in Beckett's Run. The same things, with the same people, every day. When he'd been a kid, he'd hated that. A part of him missed the hustle and bustle of Boston, the friends he met for an after-dinner beer and watching the game on the big screen. He missed having his own space, his own sofa, his own bed. Staying with his mother was definitely a temporary plan. Still, there was something about this town, something so basic, the kind of thing people built foundations on and lives on. Every time he was here, it was like he was...

Home.

Maybe he should think about making a more permanent stamp on the place. Hell, half the time he was here more than in the city. He shook his head. Who was he fooling? He wasn't the settling down kind. He had a busy, demanding company and a life in Boston. A sometimes-girlfriend living in the Back Bay. And a whole lot of people depending on him keeping the company running and profitable.

The problem was, J.C. had already made his money, and didn't give a damn about making more. He wasn't lacking in work.

But in purpose, yeah.

He thought of the changes his family's life had taken in the last few months. The forty-pound reason he'd come back to Beckett's Run, and that had him living in his old room even though a part of him would rather be in the spacious king bed in Boston. The same reason that had him considering chucking it all and staying here.

"What are you? An idiot? Throw away a company like that? If you did, you'd be nothing."

There were days when his father's voice rang loud and clear in J.C.'s head, even though John Senior had been gone for four years. His father, a stern, brooding, unforgiving man, who had expected his son to take the helm of the family company and multiply it tenfold.

"You take care of your family by providing for them. Not doing something foolish like slaughtering the golden goose."

If J.C. stepped down from the financial management company that two prior generations of Carsons had built it would probably survive, certainly keep going. But it wouldn't be the same. How many clients had said they invested with Carson Investments because they had a personal relationship with J.C. or with his father? When it came to money, people wanted trust, and trust came from relationships.

The problem was that there were days when J.C. had to wonder whether he was pursuing the right things. At some point his own dreams and goals had gotten swallowed in the quest to expand, grow, become all he'd been tasked with being. But if he walked away—

Would he hurt or help those he loved?

J.C. heard a curse from behind him. He turned to find Grace McKinnon standing in the doorway of the coffee shop, her hair windblown from the winter air, her cheeks red and her gloved hands clutching a bag from a local bookstore.

"They're here," she said.

"Who?"

Grace jerked her gaze up to his. Those same fiery hazel eyes he remembered, the kind that could hold a man's gaze for an hour. He wondered what she was doing in town—and why she was still here. He hadn't seen her in years, and now he'd seen her twice in the space of a couple days.

"What did you say?" Grace said to him.

"You said, 'They're here.' Who did you mean?"

"Grandma's book club." Grace gestured toward the group at the back. "She said they probably wouldn't show because it was the holidays and everyone was busy."

"I can't remember a Tuesday they've missed. Well, except when they were reading one of their books and Mrs. Brimmer got into a scuffle with Miss Watson about a particularly offensive passage." J.C. grinned at the memory of being called over to settle the literary dustup. "For retirees, they can get pretty rowdy."

"Rowdy. My grandmother's book club." Grace snorted. "Right."

J.C. stepped to the right. "See for yourself."

A burst of laughter rose up again in the group, followed by the rise and fall of excited voices. Mrs. Brimmer slapped the arm of the chair she was sitting in to emphasize her point, and Mrs. Simmons got to her feet to argue it back. Their voices rose louder, over the music coming from the sound system, as the two sides voiced their opinions.

Grace groaned. "Why am I doing this?"

"You're running Mary's book club? How did that come about?"

"She asked me. And she didn't play fair." Grace leaned in closer. "She baked cookies."

When Grace closed the distance between them, J.C. bit back a groan. Damn, what perfume was that? And why did it affect him so? The dark vanilla notes lingered in the air, teasing, tempting. Overriding common sense. "Let me guess. Peanut butter blossoms?"

"And chocolate chip. The ones with the big hunks of chocolate, not those weakling little chips."

J.C. chuckled and his stomach rumbled. He'd known Mary McKinnon nearly as long as he'd known Grace. Mary's cooking far surpassed anyone's in town, and her desserts…people talked about them for years. "You're right. Your grandmother doesn't play fair."

"No, she doesn't." Grace shook her head. She pulled out a copy of Jane Austen's *Persuasion* from her purse. "Any chance you've read this book? And want to talk about it?"

"Couldn't do it even if I wanted to. I have to get to a meeting."

"Come on, J.C., help me out." She put out a hand, as if she was going to touch him, then pulled it back. "Those ladies like you. Look, they're waving."

Indeed, Mrs. Brimmer was sending J.C. a friendly

wave, and Mrs. Horton was shooting him a friendly smile. Both women had single daughters—and an eye for an eligible, employed male. "They just want me to marry their daughters."

Grace turned toward him. Surprise lit her face. "I thought you married what's-her-name."

"I didn't." He left it at that. No need to rehash a long personal history, one Grace hadn't been around to witness.

"Oh." She bit her lip, which he knew—too well—meant she was biting back a few words. "I should probably get to the book club and talk about…" She turned the bag over in her hands. "Whatever it is that happens in this book."

"Did you read it?"

"Heck, no. But I looked it up online and got a plot outline. Jane Austen, trying to fix up everyone in the boring little town where she lives. Happy ending. Done."

He chuckled. "Wow. Speed reader." Then he leaned in toward her. He told himself it was to keep their conversation private, but then he inhaled, and knew it was really an excuse to catch a whiff of that perfume again. "And speed driver."

"This town can't plow its roads. It's not my fault I slid."

"You've been to Beckett's Run enough times to know not to speed in the winter. And in a car like that, no less. Don't blame the town for your recklessness."

She perched a fist on her hip. "Are you calling me reckless?"

"Aren't you?"

Grace bit her lip again, then shook her head. "You haven't changed at all, J.C. Carson. Not one bit."

"Oh, I've changed, Grace, more than you know." He

shot her a grin, then turned toward the door. "Have fun with the book club. And don't let Jane Austen get to you. Just because she believed in happy endings doesn't make her wrong. They do happen. For lots of people." Then his gaze met hers, and a wave of memories surged forward. Memories that tasted of honey and lemon, sweet and bitter, memories that haunted his nights and whispered *what-ifs* every time he saw her. Memories that would do nothing but open a door he had sealed shut a long time ago. "Just not for you and me."

CHAPTER THREE

GRACE tried to concentrate. Tried to pay attention to the women around her. But her mind kept straying to J.C.

He'd aged well. Very well. Still had the same deep blue eyes and short dark hair as always, but there was an added ruggedness to his features, a depth to his face, that spoke of loss, experience. A part of her wanted to sit on the banks of the creek with him, watching the minnows dart around their feet in silver arrows while she and J.C. talked until they could talk no more. Another part warned that everything between she and J.C. was over, in the past—

Where it should stay.

He'd left after their brief conversation this morning, letting in a burst of chilly air as he exited the coffee shop. Leaving his last comment hanging, like some mystery waiting to be solved.

She already knew the answer.

Years ago, she and J.C. had been inseparable. Two peas in a pod, her grandmother had called them. He'd been the one bright spot in her miserable summers spent in Beckett's Run, the one thing she'd looked forward to every time her mother dumped her and her sisters on Gram's front porch and left so fast the dust didn't even have time to settle in the driveway.

Then J.C. had dumped her, the whole event cold, heartless, cowardly, and it ended just like that. She'd left Beckett's Run—and never looked back.

Until now.

"I think the persuasion part of the novel was all about Anne trying to persuade women to be stronger," Mrs. Brimmer said, drawing Grace back to the book club. "She was a regular feminist, that Anne."

"Are you completely daft, Pauline? Anne caves to conventionality in the end. Why, she takes three steps back for the women's movement." Miss Watson shook her head, and several gray strands escaped from the messy bun on top of her head. "Makes me glad I never got married. I wouldn't want some man making all the decisions."

"I would disagree," Mrs. Brimmer said. "Anne is one of the strongest women I've ever seen in a book."

Miss Watson huffed. And puffed. "Strong women don't settle down with spineless men."

"Captain Wentworth is far from spineless. He encourages Anne to be strong and independent. Much like my dear Harvey did with me." Then Mrs. Brimmer swung her attention toward Grace. She leaned her tall frame forward, and put one bony hand on Grace's arm. "Tell us, Grace, what do you think? You're part of the younger generation. What did you think of Anne?"

"Me? I…" She glanced down at the book in her lap, the spine as pristine as it had been on the shelf at the bookstore. The internet hadn't given her a ready-made opinion. "Well, I didn't exactly have time to form a concrete judgment about her."

"You didn't read the book?" A collective gasp went up from the group. "Any of it?"

"Well, no, I mean, my grandmother just told me about this and—"

"But, dear, Jane Austen is required reading for any woman who wants a happy ending of her own." Mrs. Horton's hand landed on Grace's other arm. "Her novels are like…well, a guide to finding true love."

Several "amens" went up from the other women. A chorus of Austen recommendations started up, with each of the book club members tossing out their pick for top romantic guide by the famed writer. "Mary told us that you haven't settled down yet," Miss Watson said. "She's set us all on a mission of sorts, too."

Mrs. Brimmer smacked Miss Watson's arm. "Shut your trap."

"Mission?" Grace put the book aside. Alarm bells clanged in her head. "What mission?"

Miss Watson glanced at Mrs. Brimmer, who shook her head. "Oh…nothing. Just an idea she had. You know us old ladies. We're always looking for something to do."

"That's why we have *book club,*" Mrs. Brimmer said, stressing the last two words. "So we talk about books, and nothing else."

Miss Watson nodded. "Okay, back to Jane. And Anne."

Grace agreed. Being one half of someone's match-making equation wasn't on her agenda. Now or later. Her grandmother didn't really expect these women to find Grace a happy ending, in the next few days, did she? Gram knew Grace would never want to settle down here. What was she thinking?

The coffee shop door opened and a trio of people walked inside. A man in a suit and tie, trailed by a young man and woman, both scruffy in stonewashed jeans, oversize anorak jackets and sturdy boots. "Oh, Lordy,

it's Carlos Fitz from the local news," Mrs. Brimmer exclaimed. "If I was twenty years younger—"

"You'd still be old enough to be his mother," Miss
Watson cut in. "Do you think they're here about the
celebration?"

"What celebration?" Grace asked, playing dumb.
Often the best information came if one pretended one
didn't know anything. She was half tempted to get out
her notebook and start jotting notes, but figured that
would be obvious. At Gram's house she had read the
local paper's accounts of the event, and done a cursory
internet search, but hadn't really found anything that
leapt out as a career-saving story yet.

"Why, the Christmas one we have every year," Mrs.
Brimmer answered. "Two hundred years this year."

"And you remember every last one," Miss Watson
quipped.

Mrs. Brimmer went on, ignoring her friend. "Didn't
you know Beckett's Run was named 'Most Christmas
Spirit' by that magazine?"

Grace glanced back at the trio from the television station. That meant the media had already latched on to the
Beckett's Run event. She needed to come up with her
own unique angle if she was going to impress her editor. "So who's in charge of this celebration?"

"J.C. Carson." Mrs. Brimmer let out a sigh. "Why,
he's been a one-man wonder, getting this town back on
its feet in the last few months, thank the Lord. The place
looks amazing, don't you agree?"

Grace nodded. She'd noticed shiny benches, repainted
storefronts, jaunty awnings all over the place. There
were also several new green spaces and walking paths
dusted by fresh snow. "Downtown is gorgeous. Looks
brand-new."

"That's because it is, all thanks to J.C. and his Beckett's Run renovation project. This town is lucky to have him around." The other women nodded agreement, and several sang J.C.'s praises, painting him both as a hero and savior.

Grace swiveled back to the women. "You said J.C. is in charge of the Winter Festival?"

"Yep. Doing a bang-up job, too. Even if the volunteers on his committee are letting that poor young man shoulder most of the work, especially with everything else he has going on," Mrs. Brimmer said. The other women nodded agreement." He's a trooper, I tell you. I can't wait to see what he manages to pull off this year. It should be a spectacular…"

But Grace had stopped listening. The wheels turned in her head. A national story. One with a little heart, and a financial twist. She got out of her seat. "I have a call to make. I'll see you all next Tuesday."

She hurried out of the coffee shop, tugging her cell out of her jeans pocket as she did. Just before the door shut she heard Mrs. Brimmer call out, "You left your book behind! You'll never know how it ends!"

Grace let the door shut. She didn't care about the fictional ending created by Austen, not when she could write a new beginning for herself.

The only roadblock? Getting J.C. Carson to cooperate.

J.C. regretted bringing the cookies. And the coffee. He'd led board meetings that accomplished more than this one. Maybe it was the small town atmosphere. Or maybe it was the damned cookies. "Gang, can we get to work? We've got a lot to do and not a lot of time."

Walter Westmoreland, Carla Wilson, Sandra Perkins

and her daughter Anna turned toward J.C.. "Isn't it snacktime?" Sandra asked. "If I don't eat, my blood sugar drops."

"Yeah, and then she can't concentrate," her daughter added. Both women mirrored each other in actions and looks. Red-headed buns, cashmere twinsets, and a complaint gene that often kicked in at the worst possible time. J.C. wondered if that came from the two of them living in such close quarters for so long. Sandra was in her eighties, her daughter only twenty years younger, and a permanent roommate for her long-widowed mother. They did everything together, including this committee.

Walter was only here at Sandra's behest. There'd been an on-again, off-again romance between the two for as long as J.C. could remember. Much to the objections of Anna, who wasn't in the Walter Westmoreland Fan Club.

J.C. could have paid professionals from the outside to come in and handle the entire event, start to finish, but that would have given the Winter Festival a canned feel. The "Most Christmas Spirit" moniker had come about because the magazine liked the town feel of Beckett's Run, the way people pitched in and helped out. If J.C. had come in with his checkbook and his polished experts, he would have eaten away at the very heart of the Beckett's Run Winter Festival. He didn't want to do anything that would hurt the festival's chance of success.

Especially this year. This year mattered more than any in the two hundred previous, at least to J.C.

So he had stepped up as leader and accepted help from the locals. And tried not to grumble too much.

"You have all the cookies you want, my dear," Walter said, handing Sandra a full plate.

"Bring the cookies to the table," J.C. said, "and we can get to work while we eat."

"If I talk while I eat I get indigestion." Walter scowled.

J.C. bit back a sigh. He loved this town, he really did, but there were days... "Okay, a few more minutes. And while you're eating, I was hoping one of you would volunteer for the publicity job. Louise had to step down because her grandson is sick, so I need someone else to head that up."

"I'll do it."

J.C. pivoted toward the familiar voice. Grace Mc-Kinnon stood in the doorway of the community center, her cheeks flushed from the cold. She looked beautiful and cold all at once, her hair up in the familiar ponytail, and a thick blue jacket turning her curves into a shapeless pouf. Still he knew—oh, he knew—what an amazing body lay beneath that damned coat. He cursed his hormones for reacting when his heart knew to avoid her. "What are you doing here?"

"Volunteering." She put a smile on her face and strode forward. "I heard you needed help, so here I am."

"You? Helping promote Beckett's Run?"

"Of course." She picked up a cookie and took a bite.

"You." It wasn't even a question this time.

"Me." She gave him a grin. "So where do I start?"

"Right here," Sandra said, patting one of the chairs that ringed the table. "We could use another helping hand. J.C. is working us to the bone."

J.C. begged to differ. But he did what his mother had always told him to do—kept his mouth shut until he had something nice to say—and took a seat at the head of the conference table. Grace slipped into the chair offered by Sandra, and the rest of the group trudged over to the table. He called the meeting to order, and started running down his list of topics.

His mind remained, though, on Grace. Why was she here? Not just at the meeting, but in town? After she'd turned eighteen she'd hit the road and ever since avoided Beckett's Run like the plague. Never much of a fan of the town to begin with, she'd once told him she'd never return. She liked the life of freedom that freelancing gave her. No ties to any one place or person.

It had been the final lynchpin in their relationship. He'd had to make a choice, and though it had broken his heart at the time he'd had to face the reality that Grace would never want the life he did. She hadn't been there the one day he'd needed her, and that had told him more than any conversation on the creek ever had. Grace had been far away, already embarking on her life of adventure—

Leaving him behind as fast as she could.

The familiar hurt from that day resurged in his chest. Once upon a time he'd thought she cared about him. Really cared. But when it came right down to it, she hadn't cared about anyone but herself. Damn. Why did that still affect him all these years later?

Now she was here, and volunteering for a committee, for a task that would benefit the town she hated so much. One that would tie her down, through the celebration and maybe for a few days afterward with post-publicity. This, from a woman who wanted no connections? Why?

He wanted to decline her help but had to admit that having an experienced journalist on his side would be a boon. He'd been half-assing the publicity himself, along with Louise Tyler, who meant well but knew little about media. He'd had a couple meetings with a Boston marketing firm, looking for advice, but all their recommended approaches had felt more New York than small town. Keeping the publicity local was the best and only choice. After all, who knew the town better than those who lived here, who loved this place?

But Grace? She didn't fit either criteria. Maybe this was a mistake. Either way, he didn't have time to bring another person up to speed.

"Okay, so our first big day, as you all know, is the day before Christmas Eve. There'll be festivities all week leading up to that, with the grand finale on the twenty-fourth." J.C. scanned the paper then updated the group on various volunteer activities. Anna and her mother agreed to stay on top of the food donations, while Walter stepped up to coordinate the kick-off parade. Carla, organist at the local Lutheran church, offered to spearhead the musical acts. Across from him, Grace scribbled notes on a slim pad of paper. She asked few questions, but seemed to keep track of everything said.

The meeting began to break up, with Walter and Sandra heading out first, followed closely by Anna. Carla hurried past them to pick up her son from preschool. J.C. gathered up his notes and crossed to the other side of the table.

"I was thinking we should take more advantage of social media," Grace said, her gaze on the notebook, filled with her familiar tight scrawl. "Use them to spread the word to communities outside of ours. And sometimes things like that get picked up by other media outlets. Before you know it, this could go international."

"Good idea. Something I kicked around but haven't had time to do."

Grace tapped her pen against her lower lip. "I was also hoping to profile a few local residents. Those who remember Christmas in years gone by. Maybe some of the ladies from the book club or another resident who has a heartwarming memory or story. If I can make this event have heart, it'll create a connection with the readers."

All business. Which was what J.C. had told himself he wanted. But his mind kept drifting from the project at hand to the woman inches away. A woman he hadn't seen in over a decade, and who was now plugged into the town like a peg in a fencepost.

"Why are you really here?" he asked Grace.

"Because you needed help." She got to her feet, the notebook clutched against her chest like an armor plate. "The ladies at the book club said you've been pretty much single-handedly running this thing for weeks."

"Since when do you help me?"

"We've always been friends, J.C., haven't we?"

Friends. Yes, they'd been friends. And much more for a while. Much, much more. A part of him missed that—the part that clearly had no common sense, because getting involved with Grace McKinnon was like attaching his heart to a runaway train.

He wanted to refuse her help. Wanted to keep her away from him. Wanted to stem the tide of memories that rushed to the forefront every time he saw Grace. He'd thought they were over, that he no longer cared about her. Then she'd roared into town in that impractical car and confirmed what he already knew—

He hadn't forgotten her. Not at all. And the part of him that wanted to keep her far away got overruled by the part that had never been able to resist the allure of the wild rush that was Grace McKinnon. "You're right, I have been handling a lot of this myself. And I can use every bit of help I can get. Ever since the magazine did that story, the simple Christmas festival has mush-roomed into a giant event."

She smiled, and the wattage of her smile hit him hard. "Looks like we'll be working together," Grace said. "I hope you're okay with that."

He took a step closer to her, so close he could see the flecks of gold in her eyes, catch the whiff of that damnable perfume again and feel the slight whisper of her breath on his skin. "I'm okay with it. The question is whether you are."

She lifted her chin to his in that defiant gesture he knew too well. "I am not here to open old doors, J.C., just to get through the holidays."

"And move on again?"

"That's what I do. It's my job."

"No, it's your personality. Never stay too long. Never connect too much. Never think twice about what, or who, you left behind."

She shook her head and looked away. "That's not true."

"Then prove it, Grace, and stay till the end."

"The end of what?"

"Of whatever happens here. Don't run out the door the minute it opens." What the hell was he doing? Challenging her to a date? Picking up where they left off? Maybe more?

Hell, he knew better than that.

She glanced away, and he knew he'd read her right. Grace wasn't here to stay. She never had been, and that brief moment when he'd caught the whiff of her per-fume and been tempted all over again had passed. He'd get through this event, keep it his top priority, and avoid Grace as much as possible. "I appreciate whatever help you can give to the festival." He turned toward the door. "It means a lot to the town."

She laid a hand on his arm. "J.C.?"

He pivoted back, and even though her hand dropped away the imprint of her touch remained, heat on his skin. "Yeah?"

Another smile curved across her face, the smile he had once memorized. There'd been a time when she had smiled at him like that, and his world had spun on its axis. Even now, years later, his heart leapt and filled with hope. *Damn.*

"How about cutting me a break and leading that book club for my grandma? Those ladies really seem to like you," she said.

Disappointment bloomed inside him. When was he going to learn? Grace didn't want or need anyone but herself. Getting close to her again could only lead to disaster, bring him back down the paths he had stepped off a long time ago.

"No can do. I have a job to do, Grace. And so do you." He plucked the paper with the media contacts out of her grasp. "On second thought, I don't need your help. Beckett's Run has always gotten along just fine without you and it will keep on doing that long after you leave. Again."

CHAPTER FOUR

GRACE resisted the urge to march after J.C. and tell him where he could stick his thoughts about her. The man grated on her nerves. Always had.

Well, that wasn't quite true. There'd been a time...

A long time ago. Better forgotten.

She tucked her notepad into her purse and headed out of the community center and into the bright winter sunshine. As she did, she saw J.C. standing across the street, talking on his phone.

Damn, he was a good-looking man. Taller now than she remembered from her teenage years, and stronger, more...masculine. He had an almost predatory leanness about him, a caged panther with tense muscles and unspent energy. Heat unfurled in her belly, reawakening the deepest parts of her. The parts that remembered. Oh, how they remembered J.C. Carson.

And they also remembered the painful breakup. The harsh slammed door on what she'd thought were real feelings.

She thought of the notes in her purse. The article she wanted to write. The short amount of time she had left. To accomplish any of that she needed an inside view of the festival. That would give her access the other reporters didn't have. In order to get inside, though, she needed to convince J.C. she was the right person for the job. His confidence in her was shaky, something she begrudgingly understood. She had never been the kind for staying in one place.

She crossed the street, working a smile to her face. A professional, nice, work-with-me smile. One that she prayed didn't betray any of the riot in her gut. "J.C. Got a minute?"

He nodded, put up a finger, then turned back to the cell. "Shoot me the numbers by the end of the day, Charles. I'll look them over and get back to you." He paused, then his brows knitted with frustration. "Yes, I'll be at those meetings, but I won't be back in the office for good until after the first. The company will be fine until then." Another pause, some more brow-scrunching, then finally J.C. said goodbye and tucked the phone away. "Sorry about that," he said to Grace.

"The pesky day job?"

"You could say that. They're not supposed to be calling me this week. I'm on…vacation."

"You took a vacation here? In the middle of winter? Why not some sandy beach with a blonde and a margarita?"

"I'm not the margarita type."

He didn't answer the blonde part, and Grace caught herself running a hand over her own light locks. Damn him. He kept distracting her. She no longer cared if he preferred blondes or brunettes or if he was married or single.

Didn't care at all.

Then why did she curse silently when she noticed his hands were gloved—and the question about his marital status would have to wait for an answer?

"I wanted to talk to you some more about the event,"

she said. Focus on the story, so she could redeem her career and get the heck out of Beckett's Run before Gram hosted a full-out McKinnon family reunion.

"I told you. I don't need your help."

She propped a fist on her hip. "Don't be stubborn, J.C. Let me help. I'm the expert in this and you know it."

"If I say yes," he said, taking a step closer, "then I have to know that you're going to stick with the job and not leave just because the wind started blowing in another direction."

Was that how he saw her? God, she sounded like her mother. She wasn't like that. At all. Okay, maybe a little. "I'm here until Christmas. Besides, I promised my grandmother, so that means I definitely won't leave."

Although she'd been contemplating doing that very thing, if only to avoid seeing her sisters. J.C. didn't need to know that, though.

"And you'd never break a promise to Gram, would you?" he asked. Implied, unsaid—she would break a promise to him.

"I'm here till Christmas," she repeated. "And since the festival ends on Christmas Eve, that works out perfectly."

His gaze met hers and held for a long moment. "Okay." He reached into his coat pocket and withdrew the list of media contacts, handing them over to her.

"Thanks. You can count on me, J.C."

"Can I?"

They had stopped talking about the festival and publicity and articles a long time ago, if they ever had been. Long-ago hurts popped up like stubborn moles between them. "Yes, J.C., you can. Even I grew up, too." She broke the eye contact and cleared her throat. "Anyway, since we're on a tight time schedule, I wanted to ask you a few questions to help me get a good handle on it for the publicity. Do you have some time to chat?"

He flipped out his watch. She'd expected a fancy designer brand, but J.C.'s wrist sported a plain old watch. "I've got an appointment to get to. I won't be free until later. Can we talk on the phone tonight? Or make an appointment tomorrow?"

She laughed. "Look at you. All scheduled and organized. I bet you even have some tidy little planner to keep track of every minute."

"What's wrong with that?"

"It's not who you are, J.C. You're the guy who would run off in the middle of a hot summer day to take a swim. The guy who ditched school to go watch a drag race. The guy who—"

"I'm not that person anymore, Grace."

"Sure you are. Deep down inside, I'm sure there's a little wild man in you." But her laughter was shaky, the words unsure.

"Teenage foolishness, nothing more. Anyway, I have to get to work."

"Who the hell replaced J.C. Carson?"

"Nobody did, Grace. This is who I always was." Then he turned and left, leaving her wondering if she'd ever really known him at all.

J.C. pulled in front of Grace's grandmother's house and wondered, for the hundredth time, what had prompted him to agree to drive them downtown for Mary's hair appointment. A good chunk of his Grace memories centered around downtown Beckett's Run, which meant just being there meant taking a few steps back in time.

And retreading ground he had no intention of visiting.

But Mary had called him, and asked him to deliver her safely because "you have that S.U.V. and my car is in the shop." Mary had asked him, and J.C. loved Mary enough to say yes, no matter what.

He got out of the truck and started toward the porch. The new snowfall had left a thick coat of white on Mary McKinnon's walk and steps, so he grabbed the shovel by the door and got to work on a little snow removal. The door opened behind him.

"J.C. Carson, what do you think you're doing?"

He turned around and gave Mary a grin. "Just getting into your good graces, Mrs. McKinnon."

She laughed. "You've always been there, young man. I'd say you're angling for some of my homemade fudge."

"Is it fudge baking time again? I had no idea."

She gave him a sure-you-didn't grin, then waved toward the house. "Come on in and I'll give you an extra large helping."

"You're speaking my language, Mrs. McKinnon." J.C. leaned the shovel against the porch wall, then leaned down and bussed a kiss against Mary's cheek. He'd been over at her house so much as a kid he might as well have been a relative. There had been days when she'd felt more like his grandmother than his own grandma. The normalcy of the McKinnon house, the way Mary loved her grandkids with a simple touch, no attached expectations, had been a welcome detour from his own home.

She cupped a hand to his cheek. "You're such a sweet boy, J.C."

He chuckled. "I'd like to think I'm all grown-up now."

She waved a hand in dismissal. "To me, you'll always be a boy. And I never met a man who grew up before the age of seventy." She led the way into the house, where the scents of cinnamon and pine greeted J.C.'s nostrils.

Mary cut a piece of fudge from a pan on the kitchen table, then handed it to him.

He took the sweet treat, raised it to his mouth for a bite, then paused. Grace had descended the stairs, and paused a second to fix her hair in the mirror. He watched the unguarded moment, feeling almost guilty. She raised a hand to the long blond locks, brushing them back from her forehead.

He could count on one hand the number of times he'd seen her hair down, unfettered, loosed from its perpetual ponytail. The first time she'd been twelve, climbing a tree. A branch had snagged the ponytail, and she'd ripped out the elastic and kept on climbing. She'd looked like a wild child, hair a burst of gold around her features, as she clambered from one branch to the next, scaling one lofty perch after another.

The second time she'd been running late for some event or another that slipped his mind now, and she'd forgotten to bring an elastic. He'd been fourteen, and teased her about her model look. She'd slugged him and said he'd never see her like that again. And he didn't, not for years and years.

Until she was seventeen, and he'd asked her to the dance in the park. One of those summer events put on in Beckett's Run and, for J.C., his first official "date" with Grace. That year had been the first one he'd truly noticed her. As a young woman. As someone who made his heart race. Muddled his thoughts. He'd asked her to the dance in a stammering, halting monologue. She'd met him at the entrance to the park in a dress—another rarity for Grace—with her hair a cascade of gold along her shoulders. From that moment on he was a goner.

She pivoted away from the mirror and noticed him standing there, watching her. She reached up a hand to smooth the long locks again, then scowled. "Why are you here?"

"Because your grandmother asked me to drive her downtown."

"*I'm* supposed to go with her."

"That powder puff you're driving is useless on these roads, and we're expected to get more snow tonight. I have an S.U.V. I'm just being practical."

"Be nice to J.C., Grace," Mary added. "He did just shovel our walk."

The scowl edged into a smile. "Trying for brownie points, Mr. Carson?"

He put the fudge on the table, then strode forward. No dress today—a pity—but she had on long sleek black jeans—skinny jeans, he thought they were called—that hugged her thighs, curved over her calves and ended with high-heeled short black boots. A V-necked red sweater emphasized the swell of her breasts, the hourglass of her waist. "Wouldn't want you to slip and fall," he said.

"And leave you without a publicist again?"

The question drew him back to the present. This wasn't a replay of that dance in the park, nor did he want it to be. It was business, town business, and he would do well to remember that. He had responsibilities, and forgetting them with Grace wasn't in the plan. "Exactly."

She parked a fist on her hip. "I can get through the snow on my own, you know."

He snorted. "In those shoes? I doubt it."

"I can do a lot of things for myself, J.C. I don't need a man taking care of me."

"Oh, I remember that. Very well." Too well. Grace had made it clear she never wanted a commitment, never wanted to be tied down, never wanted to depend on anyone but herself—and especially never wanted anyone to depend on her. The one day when he had needed her—

She'd been gone.

Proving her point to the nth degree.

Why hadn't she been there? Why had she just blown out of town, leaving him to deal by himself? In her eyes he didn't see anything other than the same honest what-you-see-is-what-you-get Grace, which didn't fit the woman who had left him in the dust.

"Fudge?" Mary inserted a platter between the two of them. "A little chocolate makes everything sweeter."

"That it does," J.C. said, selecting a second piece.

Grace took a small one for herself, and took a bite. J.C. told himself not to watch her pink lips close around the treat. Tried not to stare at the tiny dot of chocolate on her upper lip. Tried not to fantasize about kissing her until all traces of chocolate disappeared.

She hadn't changed at all—the comment a second ago reminded him of that fact—and that meant they were still as mismatched as ever. The things that had driven a wedge between them before still existed, and he'd be a fool to ignore those facts.

He cleared his throat. "We better get going."

"Gram, if J.C. is taking you, I don't have to go, too."

"Oh, he's just dropping me off. You have to come, Grace. Who else is going to make sure Jane doesn't turn me into a blue-haired pouf?"

Grace laughed. "Okay, I'll go. But just so you know I'm not exactly fashion-savvy."

Mary insisted on filling a plastic container with fudge for J.C. and making sure he took it with him as a thank-you for shoveling the walk. "I'll make sure someone plows your drive tonight, too, Mrs. McKinnon." He put up a hand. "And don't tell me I don't have to do that.

You're practically my grandma, too, so think of it as your grandson taking care of you. No dessert payment necessary."

"You're so sweet." She smiled, gave him a tender touch and the three of them headed out the door.

At the truck, J.C. helped Mary in, then reached for the back-door handle, but Grace opened it before he could, and swung herself up into the seat without any trouble. He got in on the driver's side, flipping the heat to high before putting the car in gear and heading down the street. Grace sat behind him, bundled up in a thick anorak jacket.

Mary's praise for the town's decorations and the job J.C. was doing filled the space as they made the short, chilly drive to downtown Beckett's Run. J.C. parked in the newly plowed lot that sat between Carol's Diner and the hair salon, and before he'd exited the truck Grace had already opened her door and climbed out.

Clear message—no need to be chivalrous.

Then why did he make sure he got to the salon's door first, to hold it for her? Geez, he was like a schoolboy, and that wasn't who he was. At all.

"Thanks," she said, slipping past him.

The soft notes of her perfume teased at his senses. Once again, the light scent surprised him. He'd never have picked Grace for the sweet type. She was the hard-edged, take-no-crap adventurer he knew as a kid. Of course there'd been a time when he'd seen her as someone else. Someone far more…feminine.

Mary stopped just inside the door of the salon. "Oh, my. I totally forgot."

Grace turned back. "You forgot something, Gram?"

"Tonight's my night to call bingo down at the church. I'll have to skedaddle if I'm going to be there on time."

"What about your hair appointment?"

"Oh, that. Well, I forgot that, too. It's not today. It's tomorrow. Right, Jane?" she called to the hairdresser at the back.

"You're right, Mary. Tomorrow at ten."

"Goodness, I'm getting so old I forget where I'm supposed to be half the time." She bundled her coat again and tugged a scarf over her hair. "Anyway, off to the church!"

"Let me drive you," J.C. said.

"No, no. It's only one block away. You two stay, go to Carol's, get some dinner. I'll catch up with you later. Walter will give me a ride home." Before he could protest, Mary whirled around and out the door, leaving Grace and J.C. alone.

"Well, that was obvious," Grace said, heading back out into the cold. "I've just been stood up and match-maked by my own grandmother."

J.C. chuckled. "She means well."

"She does. Anyway, thanks, J.C." She started to turn away, but he put out a hand to stop her. A momentary touch, but one that lit a fire in him.

"What about dinner? I'm hungry, and I'm sure you are, too. I'm supposed to be going to my aunt's house for horrible chicken casserole. I'd love to have a reason to miss that."

She cocked her head. "Are you using me to get out of dinner with your family?"

"Absolutely." He grinned. "Do you mind? We could go to Carol's. We're already here."

"I haven't been there in forever. Is Carol still working the counter?"

"Every Tuesday and Thursday. Her granddaughter took over the day-to-day a few years ago, but Carol likes to keep her hands in the pie, so to speak. She says it keeps her out of trouble." He leaned in closer to her, so close she caught the faint scent of his cologne. Dark, musky, male. Tempting. "And they still have the chicken pot pie you love."

"You remember that?"

"How could I forget? It was the only thing you ever ordered."

"I really liked that pie," Grace said, her voice squeaking a bit on the last syllable. Was she talking about pie? Or something else?

"I know you did. It's how we met. Do you remember?"

Her gaze met his blue eyes. Did she remember?

Of course she did. She'd been six, at the diner with her sisters and Gram, a treat to get the girls' minds off the sight of their mother's Buick heading down the street, away from them. Always away.

They'd sat at the counter, Grace, the shortest one, dangling her feet over the stool, shiny new shoes tapping the center pole of the stool. Another family had come in—mom, dad, son, daughter. She heard them telling the hostess they wanted a booth, but the diner was busy and they'd ended up reluctantly at the counter. The dad had complained, loud and long, but the kids had looked happy to have a change of scenery for dinner. The parents took the far end, the kids closest to Grace. She'd noticed the boy, but only as a fidgety body beside her. She'd been focused on jostling for space—and Gram's attention—with her sisters. Then the waitress had brought out a chicken pot pie and both she and J.C. had reached for it at the same time.

He'd given her a shy smile and withdrawn first. "It's yours," he said.

She'd thanked him, then for no reason she could re-member except maybe she wanted to avoid her sisters she'd started talking to the boy. "It's my favorite," she said.

"Mine, too." Then he threw out a hand, formal, stiff. "J.C. Carson."

She liked the way he said his name, in one mouth-ful. Her own tripped over her nervous tongue, but J.C. just smiled. "Grace," he said, and then, just like he had the other day, he'd added, "Welcome to Beckett's Run, Grace."

J.C's father had shushed him and told him to behave. In an instant the friendliness had dropped from J.C.'s face and he'd gone stone-cold and still. He hadn't said another word to her the rest of the night, but when his chicken pot pie arrived he shot her a grin, then scooped up a bite almost too big for his mouth.

"J.C., don't make an animal of yourself," his father had said. "We're in a public place, for God's sake."

"Yes, sir." J.C. dipped his head and the boy she'd met disappeared again.

She'd run into J.C. again the next day at the park, and the day after that at the town pool. She'd soon re-alized there were two J.C.s—the one under his father's thumb and the one who wanted to wriggle out as fast as he could.

The latter had been the J.C. she had fallen for. But it had been the other J.C.—cold, analytical, practical—who had broken her heart.

They had history. Something she kept having trou-ble ignoring. She thought of the article she was work-ing on. That was her ticket out of this hellhole and back to the life she loved. She wasn't going to go back down Memory Lane with J.C. They'd broken up for a reason, even if she forgot that reason when he looked at her like that.

"That was a long time ago," she said finally. "Pretty much a distant memory now. I'd much rather focus on the present. So if we go to dinner it's to talk about the Christmas celebration."

"Good idea." He led the way the few feet over to the diner, then held the door for her. The diner was crowded, filled with locals looking for a warm meal and a warm place on the chilly winter night.

He cleared his throat. "A booth in the back okay with you? It can get rowdy in here sometimes."

Grace laughed as she followed behind him, weaving their way in and out of the tables and toward the back of the room. "Honey, you haven't seen rowdy until you've been in some seedy bar in Mexico at two in the morning." Then she colored as if she realized she had called him honey. "*That's* rowdy. This is…"

His gaze met hers. "This is what?"

"Safe. Dependable." She mocked a yawn. "Boring."

"Which is exactly why you ran out of here so fast the dust is still settling in your wake?"

"I was never going to live here, J.C. You knew that."

"And where do you live now? Did you settle down in Peoria with two kids and a Labrador?"

"God, no." She pulled out one of the two-sided laminated menus from behind the napkin dispenser and skimmed the offerings. "I have a very small apartment with very little furniture in a very low-rent part of New York, but I'm hardly ever there. I guess you could say I don't really live anywhere." She raised her gaze to his. "What about you? Still living on Merry Street in Beckett's Run? Or did you move to the big city and make your mark on the world?"

"I have a house in the city, and plan on going back there soon. For now, I'm living here, and, yes, back on Merry Street. At my mom's house."

"You're living in Beckett's Run? Why?"

"I have...personal business to attend to here." He left out the specifics. Grace and he were no longer an item, and that meant he didn't need to involve her in his family messes.

Still, a part of him—the part that still remembered long walks down to the creek where they'd chased toads and caught crayfish—missed talking to Grace. She'd been everything his home life had never been—fun, unfettered, spontaneous. Those hot summer days with her had been the highlight of his school vacation. No expectations, no rules. Just some water, mud and a lot of laughter.

That was what he remembered most about those summers. The laughter. The fun. The reckless chances. How long had it been since he'd had days like that?

Forever.

He had grown up, which meant he had responsibilities—one very big one right now in his life—and yearning for what used to be was an exercise in futility.

"I had personal business here, too," Grace said. "Seems no matter how hard we try to escape Beckett's Run, it keeps sucking us back in, huh?"

"Maybe I'll end up settling down here, if my current plan doesn't work out."

"You. Live here." She laughed. "Right. You hated this place as much as I did, J.C."

"I never hated the town. I hated..." He looked away. How had the conversation gone down this road? He was supposed to be here to talk about the town celebration, not about himself. As many times as Grace had pressed when they'd been younger, he'd never told her what it was like to grow up as John Carson's son. J.C. knew Grace had an inkling, but he'd never shared the whole truth. His time with Grace had been a sacred escape, one he'd hated to sully.

"Doesn't matter," he said finally. "All that's in the past. I'm here to work on this Christmas celebration, and help it take Beckett's Run up to the next level."

"Hey, J.C., good to see you again. What can I get you?" A tall woman in a bright white apron clicked out a pen and order pad. Her gaze went from J.C. to Grace. They both ordered chicken pot pies and water.

Once the waitress was gone, Grace's features shifted from inquisitive to serious. She straightened in her seat, dug out the same pad he'd seen before and clicked a pen. "Why is it so important that the festival take Beckett's Run to the next level?"

He segued into business mode, too. "Because the town has been hard hit by the economy lately," he said, speaking slow at first, until he saw her handwriting flying across the page almost as fast as the words left his mouth. "And I think the town could use this economic boost. We aren't on the ocean, so we don't get much of the summer tourism dollars. However, we do have that quintessential New England feel, which is perfect for a holiday celebration. More and more families are looking for destinations for the winter months, and events they can attend with their children. My goal is to get people to visit Beckett's Run when the leaves start to change, then come back throughout the fall and winter months as a family getaway."

She raised her gaze to his. "So it's just about money?"

He bristled. "Of course not."

"Well, then, tell me why again, in a way that doesn't sound like bottom lines and dollars."

He took in a deep breath, and let his gaze wander to the snow falling outside, the townspeople bustling down Main Street on their way to shops, friends, families. There was just something about Christmas that wrapped Beckett's Run in a world of…possibilities. A mask for reality, perhaps, or maybe that lingering hope that stuck with a person long after tragedy had disrupted their dreams. "I want to give that Christmas experience to the people of Beckett's Run, and to those on the outside looking in, to help them…" he paused, thinking of one person in particular who needed this gift more than anyone he knew "…believe in magic again."

A soft smile stole across Grace's face as she wrote his words on the pad. She raised her gaze to his, the smile lingering. "That's perfect. It'll sell the whole world on coming here in the future for Christmas."

He scowled. "I'm not trying to sell the whole world. Well, I am, in a way, but…" He let out a curse and shook his head.

"What? If it's not about the whole world, then what is it about?"

His gaze went to the snow again. "That's personal."

She let out a gust. "Gee, for a minute there I thought I was talking to someone other than J.C. Carson. But clearly I wasn't." She flipped the pad closed and clicked off the pen. "If you want someone who will write something with all the personality of an ad for laundry detergent, then find another publicist. I'm not your girl."

"You never were my girl," he said. He paused, then exhaled. "Sorry. That's the past and we're not going there."

"No, we're not." She bit her lip, and when she did that

he was rocketed back a half dozen years to the Grace he used to know, the wild, untameable spirit who had climbed trees and bucked rules and dreamed of traveling the world. The woman who had once inspired him to do the same, and for a moment he'd been close—so close—to having the dreams he'd wanted. Then reality had smacked J.C. hard and he'd realized responsibilities came with a price.

"I think this was a mistake," she said, as if she'd read his thoughts.

"We're just talking, Grace. Nothing more."

"Nothing?" She leaned forward, elbows propped on the table. "I'd say there's always been something between us."

"There used to be. There isn't anymore." But as he said the words his gaze went to her lips, then to her eyes. Something familiar stirred in his gut.

Something he didn't have time or room in his life for. As far as he was concerned that something had died. And would stay dead.

She was still the same wild child, and he couldn't afford to be that anymore. He'd become the one everyone depended upon to be responsible, grown-up, smart. Responsible men didn't run off with a vagabond writer. Smart men didn't entertain thoughts of taking her to bed. Grown-up men didn't revisit a crazy past.

"You've changed," she said, wagging the pen at him. "It's not just the fancy car and the sudden altruistic nature."

"I grew up, Grace. People tend to do that."

"You're more…uptight. You used to be fun, J.C. Adventurous."

"I'm fun." Though even as he said the words he wondered how true they were. Could he count the occasional ski trip as fun? Two trips in the last five years, both of which had been centered around business, not breaks? Those weren't fun. They were networking. Yeah, he went out with his friends from time to time, and dated off and on, but he wouldn't call anything he'd done since he left Beckett's Run *adventurous.* "It's different when you're an adult. There are…responsibilities."

"Like a wife and kids?"

Was she asking because she cared? Or because she was testing his answers? "No wife." He left off the second answer. He had no good way to answer that question without digging deep into that personal pit that he'd vowed to avoid. "What about you? Still as fun and adventurous as always?" he asked, using her words.

She looked away, then tucked the pad into her purse. "This isn't going to work, J.C. I'm sorry. I'll find you someone else."

He reached for her before she could rise. When their hands connected a familiar charge ran through him, sparking memories, desire, and want for the very thing he could never have. J.C. let go. "Don't run again, Grace."

Fire roared in her eyes, a sudden rush of the old Grace back again. "I'm not running."

"Really? Because last I remember that was your specialty. Every time someone gets close, you speed out of here." Damn. He hadn't meant to say that. What was it about Grace McKinnon? Every time he got around her it was either fireworks or firebombs. He needed to get back on track, back to the subject at hand.

The success of the Beckett's Run Winter Festival.

The waitress dropped off their order, and rather than talk to each other Grace and J.C. dug in. Across from him, Grace took a bite, then paused, a smile on her face. "As good as I remember."

"Some things never change," he said.

"And some things do," she said.

He pushed his pie to the side. "Why don't we start over again? And focus on the event instead of—"

The diner door opened and his mother walked in, an apologetic look on her face. Before J.C. could respond, a three-foot-tall bundle beelined across the restaurant and plowed his four-year-old frame into J.C.'s chest. "I wanna stay with you, not G'ma."

Across from J.C., Grace's brow had raised in a question. J.C. ignored that for now and bent down to Henry's little face. "I'm no fun, buddy. Grandma is the one with the cool toys."

Henry cupped a small hand around his mouth. "But she doesn't like to play trucks. She wants to play Barbie." He grimaced. "I don't like dolls."

J.C. raised his gaze to his mother's. She shrugged, but he could read a hundred emotions flickering in her pale blue eyes. The toys she had pulled from the attic had been mostly her daughter's, and J.C. bet those toys came with a lot of bittersweet memories. His mother's smile faltered.

"I'm sorry," she said, leaning down and placing a hand on Henry's back. "I'm trying, but sometimes it's just…"

"It's okay, Mom. I'll watch him."

She hesitated, sending Grace a distracted hello before returning her attention to J.C. "Are you sure?"

"No problem. I'll be home in a little while, and tuck him into bed, too. Okay?"

Relief flooded her features. "Okay. Thank you, J.C." She said goodbye to Henry, and headed out the door.

When his mother was gone, J.C. tipped Henry's chin toward his own. "Why don't you stay with me, buddy? I'll get the waitress to bring you an ice cream sundae, and then we'll go for a walk in the park after we eat."

"Ice cream? But it's cold outside." Henry giggled. How nice it was to hear that little boy's laugh. J.C. realized he'd do about anything to hear that sound. "Nobody eats ice cream when it's cold."

"Sure they do. It's how all the best snowmen keep their figures." J.C. grinned, then danced a finger on Henry's nose. Henry laughed again. "And you, my little snow buddy, are turning into a snowman right before my eyes."

Henry's eyes widened. "I am?"

"You are. You spend enough time outside to get the nickname of Frosty. All the more reason to keep your hat and gloves on when I take you to the park."

"Are you really going to take me?" Henry's smile flipped into a frown. "You promised and then we didn't go."

Guilt roared through J.C. He hated being the cause of the disappointment in Henry's eyes. But it seemed the more J.C. tried to do the right thing, the more he got pulled in the opposite direction. There were days when it felt like he wasn't doing any single thing well or right. But as he met Henry's eyes again he knew the most important thing to get right was sitting right in front of him. Especially at Christmas. And especially *this* Christmas.

"I know, buddy. I've been working a lot. Sorry. Tonight, for sure, I'll show you all the cool stuff we're setting up for the Winter Festival."

"Okay." Henry nodded, then climbed onto the seat beside J.C., perching on his knees and propping his chin on his hands. He turned toward Grace, and tapped a finger on J.C.'s shoulder. "You're talking to a stranger."

J.C. laughed. "Oh, this is my good friend, Grace. She's not a stranger. She just hasn't been around here lately." He gestured toward Grace, who had watched the whole exchange bemused, curious. "Grace McKinnon, I'd like you to meet Henry. Part-time snowman, full-time troublemaker."

"Hey! I'm not trouble." Henry pouted.

J.C. ruffled his hair. "Nah, you're not at all, pardner."

Grace shook hands with Henry, who gave her back the enthusiastic hand clench of a four-year-old just learning his social graces. "Pleased to meet you, Mr. Henry."

Henry beamed. "Do you like ice cream?"

"More than I like anything." Grace smiled. "Your dad's a big fan of ice cream, too. His favorite is chocolate chip, if I remember right."

"Oh, I'm not…" J.C. put up a hand to correct Grace, then let the same hand rest on Henry's narrow shoulders, like a shield.

"My mommy and daddy went to heaven," Henry supplied, his gaze on his clasped hands. His voice was soft, fragile. "They can't come back for Christmas or my birthday or anything." He heaved a sigh too big for someone so small. "I really miss them. And sometimes I talk to them, 'cept I don't think they hear me, cuz they never talk back."

Grace's hazel eyes filled with sympathy. Her gaze darted to J.C., who gave a long, slow nod. "Oh, God, I'm so sorry. I had no idea."

"*This* is why I'm in Beckett's Run, Grace. And this is why the Winter Festival is so important to me. It's not about money, or fame, or even the town, when you come right down to it. It's about this." He scooped Henry up against him, settling his nephew on his hip. "Come on, buddy. Let's get you that ice cream."

CHAPTER FIVE

J.C...A TEMPORARY father?

Grace sat in the booth at Carol's and watched him prop his nephew onto a stool at the counter, then order the largest ice cream sundae Grace had ever seen. J.C. scooped the little boy back onto one hip, grabbed the ice cream with his free hand, then returned to the table and settled Henry into the booth beside him.

Henry was a slight-framed boy in a red-and-white-striped shirt and dark jeans. He had the same dark brown hair and blue eyes as the Carsons, and Grace could also see J.C.'s sister in Henry's lopsided smile and the cowlick on the back of his head. A small boy with a broken heart. Sympathy filled Grace's heart.

"Now, let's get back to the specifics of the Winter Festival," J.C. said to her while Henry started in on his treat. "I was hoping to go over the publicity plan with you first, then tackle whatever questions you had."

All business. Just the way she liked things. Which kept her from wondering about J.C. and his nephew, and about the man she'd once known becoming a surrogate parent. If she'd been asked to name a hundred things J.C. was doing with his life, that wouldn't have even made it to the list.

She cast a glance in Henry's direction. The little boy

held the spoon in his chocolate-covered fist and scooped vanilla into his mouth, which now had a ring of chocolate that reached all the way to his nose and cheeks. "Are you sure this is a good time?"

"My schedule tomorrow is full. So, yeah, now would be good."

"Okay." She glanced again at Henry, who seemed content with his ice cream.

Grace's experience with kids could be calculated in seconds, not hours. She rarely covered family destinations for the travel magazine, and saw few children at the resorts she did visit. Her grandmother would say Grace was still a big kid herself, but there was something about being around a small child—not even interacting with him, but having him watch her with that steady, assessing, inquisitive gaze—that made Grace nervous.

"For the publicity, I'd like a multi-pronged approach," J.C. said. "Merge social media with interviews with the press, and regular updates for the website. It would be great if we could pick a few key events to focus on. Maybe the snowman-building competition and the ice-carving event."

Grace made several notes on her pad with one hand and took quick bites of pie with the other. "Do you have any food-related events? That way I could send news to the cooking blogs and food publications."

"There's a chili cook-off in the town hall tomorrow night. And an ornament-making event at the community center on…" He paused, pulled out his smartphone and scrolled through it. "Wednesday at two."

"Perfect. Do you have a photographer lined up for any or all of these?"

"Nope. Our last publicist was an all-in-one volunteer. I've been working on getting someone else, even if I have to pay for it, but it's the holidays. A hard time to find anyone. Plus, this is a town event, so people really want a town resident to be involved."

She chuckled. "Well, that eliminates me."

"You're part of this town, Grace."

"Me? Not at all," she scoffed. "I never was."

"You're more a part of this town than you know, Grace. People remember you coming here."

She shook her head. "I was a temporary visitor, and not even that in the last few years."

"There are people here who never forgot you."

She arched a brow. Did he mean himself? Or people in general? Before she could ask, she grabbed the pad of paper and refocused on her goal. "Is there anything else you wanted me to be sure I publicize?"

He leaned forward. "How are you with a camera?"

She shrugged. "Not as good as my sister, but I can do okay."

"Speaking of Hope, how is she?" J.C. asked.

"I...I don't know. I haven't seen her in a while. We're both traveling a lot, you know?" Grace jotted "photos" on her pad, dodging J.C.'s inquisitive gaze. She didn't need to go into her complicated family history, or the last fight she'd had with Hope. Or mention that Hope would be here in town soon. Best to avoid the subject all together. "We'll want to do a live play-by-play for those events on the social networking sites. I can handle that, if you want."

"That would be great. I'm trying to—"

"Do you like horses?" Henry piped up.

"Me?" Grace asked. "Uh, yeah."

J.C.'s phone rang. He mouthed an apology at Grace, then answered the call. He turned slightly away from them, keeping his voice low as he discussed something about a merger. Leaving her to interact with Henry. She dropped her gaze to her notepad and scribbled a few questions to ask J.C.

"Did you ever ride one?" Henry asked, working that chocolate ring around his mouth some more. "I wanna ride one."

Grace nodded, then put down her pen. As long as Henry was talking she wouldn't be able to get much work done. "Yes, I have. A few times."

Henry considered this. "Was it a black horse? I like black horses. They're the coolest."

Grace laughed. "Nope. Brown. No cool horses for me."

Henry turned to J.C. Melting ice cream dripped off Henry's spoon and onto the table. It spread in a pale white circle, running fast for the edge. "Uncle Jace, did you ever ride a horse?"

J.C. paused in the middle of a sentence and turned back to Henry. "Uh...what?"

"Did you ever ride a horse?" More ice cream dripped as his little hand tipped to the right, sending a large clump of vanilla onto the table. It hit with a splash, splattering ice cream onto the table, the salt shaker, and J.C.'s phone.

"I have to call you back." J.C. pressed the end button, then grabbed a few napkins and started mopping at the mess, starting with the ice cream that had landed on the phone's touchscreen. "Henry, you have to be more careful."

The little boy leaned back, away from the dripping mess. "Sorry."

J.C. sighed. "I know you are, buddy. No problem. I'll take care of it." He piled napkins on top of the mess on the table and had started to clean up Henry when his phone started ringing again. Grace could see the tension and stress in the set of J.C.'s shoulders, the shadows under his eyes.

"Go answer the call," Grace said. "I can get this."

J.C. looked at the phone's screen. "You sure? This might take a few minutes."

"That's okay." Though she had never been alone with a child before, so she wasn't so sure about that. So far Henry seemed easy enough. Talk about horses, keep him stocked with ice cream and it would all be fine. She tugged several napkins out from the dispenser and pulled them close by. Just in case.

J.C. cast one more glance at them, then answered the phone and got up from the table. He headed toward the back of the room and the relative quiet and privacy of the hall leading to the restrooms.

Grace cleaned up the rest of the ice cream mess on the table. Henry watched her, the spoon still clutched in his fist. "Hey, you…ah…need to wipe your face." She handed him some napkins.

He swiped at his lower lip, then crumpled the napkins in his hand.

"You're still a mess. Here, try again." Grace gave him another set of napkins from the tabletop dispenser.

The second time Henry scrubbed at his lips and missed the ice cream circle around his lips.

Grace laughed. She'd been the same way when she was a kid. Always messy because of some spill or adventure. "I think you need some help." She dunked a napkin into her water, then leaned forward and swiped at Henry's mouth, then used another wet napkin to wipe off his hand. He watched her work, his blue eyes wide. She wasn't sure if it was because he was scared or curious. "There, all better."

"T'ank you."

"You're welcome." Grace watched Henry finish off the sundae. At least eating kept the kid from talking to her. They'd done okay when it came to horses and ice cream, but what would she say if he asked her something like where babies came from? Or what kind of friend she was to J.C.?

"Want some?" Henry pushed the dish across to her. In five seconds he'd managed to smear ice cream all over his face again.

"Uh, no, thanks," Grace said. What was left in the glass dish had turned into a runny pale mess. "It's all yours."

"My mommy always shared. She said it was…" he thought a second for the right word "…polite."

"It is." Grace watched J.C., who was still deep into his conversation. What was she supposed to say to Henry? How was she supposed to handle this? The kid clearly missed his mother—and Grace, who had known J.C.'s younger sister, Emily, could see why. Emily had been the bubbly one of the two Carson kids. Outgoing, popular, the kind of person who smiled at everyone and never had an enemy. She would have been the kind of mom who made cookies and colored pictures.

And knew what to say when the kid brought up a tough subject.

Grace fiddled with her notes. Henry had stopped eating and was now staring at her, expectant, waiting for her to say something. "I'm…uh…sorry about your mom, kid."

Henry nodded.

"Your uncle J.C. is nice, though."

Henry nodded again.

Grace nudged the ice cream. "You going to finish that?"

Henry shook his head. "My belly's 'sploding."

"'Sploding?"

Henry puffed out his cheeks. "'Sploding."

Grace laughed. "Exploding? Oh, I bet. That's a whole lot of ice cream you ate there." She crossed her hands on the table, and figured if she could get the kid to talk about something else, he wouldn't go back to the subjects she couldn't handle. "So have *you* ever ridden a horse, Henry?"

He shook his head. "At the zoo they have ponies. And, and, I was gonna ride one, but then he made a noise, and it scared me, and I didn't."

"Was it a noise like this?" She let out a long snort sound. Henry nodded, awe on his features at her powers of intuition, or, heck, maybe just her mimicry abilities. She laughed. "The same thing happened to me when I was a little girl. I was so scared I started to cry. Maybe... it was even the same pony."

"It's a scary pony." Henry's eyes were wide, his features serious.

"Nah." Grace waved a hand. "He's just scared of you. That's why he makes all that noise, so he can make himself sound big and scary, instead of showing how worried he is about being around a big boy like you."

Henry laughed. "I'm not big."

"You are to the pony, and that's what scares him. But if you talk to him real sweet, he won't be scared of you."

"Really?"

Grace nodded. "Next time you go to the zoo, just talk nice to the pony first. Introduce yourself. Make a friend."

The happiness and excitement in Henry's features

dimmed. "I don't know when I'm gonna go to the zoo again. My mommy and daddy took me to the zoo lots. My mommy loved the zoo."

And here they were again, back at a subject that Grace had no answer to. She opened her mouth, but was saved from answering by the return of J.C. Thank God.

J.C. slid into the booth and placed the phone on the table. "Thanks."

She shrugged. "No problem."

He lowered his voice and cast a glance at Henry. "It's just been difficult. My mom tries, but she's going through her own stuff, and she's not…there like she needs to be. Anyway, thanks for the help."

Their waitress came by and cleared off the dirty dishes. "Can I get you anything else?" she asked.

"Nothing for me. Though I think we need more napkins." Grace gestured toward the empty dispenser. "J.C.'s a mess when he eats."

The waitress laughed, then laid a hand on J.C.'s shoulder. "I don't know about that." She shot him a smile of familiarity, one that sent an odd quiver of jealousy through Grace, then finished gathering the dishes. "I'll be back with more napkins and a refill of your drinks."

Grace watched her go, and tried not to hate her. Why did Grace care if J.C. had dated the waitress? The man was entitled to a life, and clearly had had one in the years since they'd broken up. She wondered why he hadn't married—after all, he'd seemed so hell-bent on settling down when she'd known him before.

His father had made it clear to her that she was far from the kind of woman J.C. wanted. *"You're a plaything, a distraction. J.C. has no intentions of anything beyond some summer fling with you so stop thinking he's going to ride off into the sunset on some crazy trip."*

In all the years she'd known J.C., she'd also known his father, and though she hadn't seen John Carson very often when she had seen him he'd offered offhand comments about how incompatible she and J.C. were. How the CEO's son would never be out and about with the flighty writer.

Maybe he'd been right. She looked at J.C. now and saw a smart, distinguished, responsible man. Even the way he carried himself screamed dependable. While she was still trekking around the world with a backpack and a passport.

"Seems the sugar high didn't last all that long." J.C. gestured toward Henry, who was curled up in the corner of the booth, his head against the soft vinyl seat, asleep. "You must have worn him out when I was on the phone."

Grace glanced at the little boy, snoring softly. Maybe she'd bored him to death. "All we did was talk about horses and ice cream."

"I appreciate it. More than you know." J.C.'s gaze held honest appreciation and gratitude.

The moment extended between them, a slowly tightening string that went from a simple thank-you to something more. Something fraught with all the unspoken history between them.

Once upon a time Grace had thought she'd run off with J.C. Carson. The two of them would blow out of this town and take on the world, Grace with her words, J.C. with his music. Then he'd changed overnight and ended their relationship without even telling her to her face, rather letting his father do the dirty work. When she'd gone to see him, to get an explanation, he'd been sitting on his porch with another girl, a girl in a frilly dress and white shoes. Grace had left Beckett's Run and never looked back.

Until now.

Damn, that day still stung, even as she told herself it didn't. She wanted to know where the other J.C. had gone, if she truly had been blinded by some crazy infatuation to the person he really was.

"Do you still play guitar?" she asked him, her dinner forgotten, the pie growing cold beside her.

"I used to. Even thought about joining a college band for one semester, but I got too busy and never did. And…" He shrugged. "Lately, I haven't had time."

"And here I thought you'd be the next big rock star."

"Yeah, well, some dreams aren't practical."

"That's the whole point of dreams, isn't it? To let you step out of the practical?"

He scoffed. "I'm as far from being an impractical dreamer as a man can get."

"Oh, I don't know about that. I bet there's some rocker in you still." That was what she was looking for, the J.C. she remembered, the man she had once fallen for. But why did she keep trying to find that side of him? Where could it possibly lead?

"If there ever was some rocker in me still," J.C. said quietly, "then the last few years have erased it completely."

He didn't elaborate, and as much as she wanted to know why she didn't press him. "That's too bad."

"Yeah," he said with a sigh. "It is."

The tension in the string between them tightened even more. Grace sensed J.C. was holding back, yet at the same time it seemed like he wanted to open up, wanted to be that boy sitting beside her on the creek bank.

She could ask, and be that friend for him again. But where would that go? In the end, she was going back to her life, and he to his. Getting close again would be a mistake. So she left the topic of his music alone and returned to the one she was here to focus on.

"Since I helped you with Henry, do you think you could repay me with a little favor?"

He arched a brow. "I know you, Grace. Your favors often get me into trouble. Grounded, or worse."

The words sent a rush of memories through her. The two of them sneaking into the closed high school one summer, just to run in the empty halls, their voices echoing off the tiled floors and walls. Then, another time, climbing the fence at the town pool after hours and taking a late-night swim. Then the day they'd cut roses from the neighbor's garden and presented them in a bouquet to Mary—not knowing the garden party was planning a tour of that garden the next morning. There'd been laughs and adventures, and something new, it seemed, every time they were together.

The memories draped over her shoulders like a blanket, comforting and suffocating all at the same time. Those memories were wrapped up in a town she wanted to forget, a town she couldn't wait to leave.

"Gram's book club is meeting again tomorrow morning," she said, returning to her purpose. Get the story and get out, with minimal personal interaction. "They're trying to wrap up the book discussion before the holiday. Come with me."

"Me? Why?"

"Because you're a good-looking man and you'll distract them from the fact that I didn't read the book."

"You think I'm good-looking?" he said. The question came with a smile, the kind of smile that teased and tempted her all at once. She glanced down, away from that smile. Damn. How did she keep ending up in this place with him?

"J.C., you know you are." She cursed the heat rising in her cheeks. Who was this shy woman? She was never shy. Never caught off guard with a man. She shot him a sarcastic grin. "It's not exactly a newsflash, Mr. Best Smile."

"Those yearbook days are a million years ago." J.C. laughed, then his gaze went to Henry and he sobered. The moment of sexual tension between them eased. "Well, I should probably get him home."

She wanted to ask him why he had stepped in as a parent. Why he was both protective and distant with his nephew. But she didn't. Instead, she glanced down at the pad of paper and refocused on her goal. She picked up the pen. "Before you go, I want to ask you a couple more questions."

"Shoot."

"You said earlier that a lot of why you are doing this Winter Festival is because of your nephew. Were you involved before that? I mean, is this an annual thing for you?"

"I've supported the town festival most years, as well as the town picnic and the summer cookout in the park. But not in as big a way as I'm doing with the Winter Festival this year. Most of my help before was financial. Donations, sponsorships, things like that. I've never been hands-on before, like I am now. In fact, you were right earlier. I used to want to be far from this town and everything it represented. Then that changed." J.C. glanced over at Henry and brushed a lock of dark hair off his nephew's head with a smooth, easy touch. Henry stirred, but didn't wake. "This year, after my sister died, I came back to Beckett's Run. At first just to help with the funeral arrangements. Then I realized my mother needed help with Henry. I thought I'd be here a few weeks at most. At the same time the Winter Festival planning began, and I realized I could be more involved than in years past. I agreed to chair it because..." his gaze again went to his nephew "...this year it's important to me that Christmas is special. Memorable. Fun."

"I understand." J.C. had surprised her yet again. Such a tender, giving thing for him to do, and here she'd been thinking he was doing all this solely to add to the Beckett's Run bottom line. Once again he showed her another side, and it intrigued her. "It must be hard to run your business in Boston and be here at the same time."

"It's challenging, to say the least." At his hip, a continual ding announced emails pouring into his phone as he spoke, all buzzing for attention. "I try to be in both places at once, and of course that's unrealistic." He sighed. "Anyway, after the Winter Festival is done I'm planning on going back to the city and back to running the investment company."

"And what will happen to Henry?"

J.C.'s gaze went to somewhere far off. He let out a long breath. "I don't know."

She could see the weight on J.C's shoulders. The decisions that were in his hands, the grief that still shimmered in his eyes. Her heart went out to him, to the man she used to know. A man she once thought she loved. But then she remembered that he had just said he was going back to the company and leaving town.

"He doesn't want that bohemian lifestyle," John Senior had said to her all those years ago. *"J.C. wants more. He just didn't know how to tell you."*

Well, J.C. had more now, and she was still that bohemian he had rejected. She needed to remember that.

His phone rang again, and he got to his feet, apologizing. "This will only take a second, I swear. If you can watch Henry—"

"No problem. Go ahead."

J.C. headed back to the hallway to talk. The waitress returned with refills for their drinks. She propped a hip against J.C.'s side of the booth and put a proprietorial hand on the back of it, as if claiming the space in his absence. "J.C. never did introduce us. I swear, that man isn't always paying attention."

Grace put out a hand. "Grace McKinnon. I don't live around here. I'm just visiting. I'm Mary McKinnon's granddaughter."

"Oh, my God! I knew you looked familiar, but it's been a long time. I'm Allie Marsh. I lived two streets away from your grandma."

"Allie, of course." Grace could see the girl she'd once known now. She barely remembered Allie, but then again that was probably because Grace had done her level best to forget Beckett's Run—at least most of it. "How are you?"

"Doing good. Still living here." Allie laughed. "I see your grandmother all the time. She comes in every Tuesday night for a piece of Carol's pecan pie. So... what are you doing with the most eligible bachelor in Beckett's Run?" The look that passed through Allie's eyes sat far on the left of friendly or inquisitive. No, she assessed Grace as if Grace was a swarm of locusts invading her land. "Heck, he's probably the most eligible bachelor in all of New England."

"J.C.?" Grace snorted. "I've known him since we were catching crayfish in the creek together. I wouldn't call him the most eligible anything."

Allie shook her head. "Honey, you must be blind or rich, or both."

"Neither." She laughed. "J.C. is still just J.C., right?"

"You have been away from town a *long* time." Allie cast a glance toward the hallway, where J.C. was still talking. "J.C. is a billionaire, or maybe he's a zillionaire by now. Why, next to Andrew Beckett, he's the best thing this town has going for it. Heck, I wouldn't be surprised if they didn't name the town square after him next year, what with all he's done for this place. Cleaning up the place, rebuilding it. He's been a godsend, that's for sure, what with so many residents struggling."

"*J.C.* has?" Grace had assumed the book club ladies had been exaggerating. Looked like she'd been wrong.

"Yup. Paid off some mortgages, bought some houses that were being foreclosed just to rent 'em back to the owners. He's helped businesses, college kids, you name it. He don't talk about it at all, of course, wants to be all anonymous, but believe me, there's no one in Beckett's Run like J.C." She said it with a mixture of admiration and infatuation. She cast a glance over her shoulder at him again. "If you ask me, the woman that lands him is going to be one lucky person. Living in the lap of luxury and waking up to him every morning." She shook her head. "Yummy."

Grace wouldn't call J.C. *yummy*. No, the words for him in her vocabulary tended more toward things like edgy, dangerous, sexy. He still had a way of looking at her and setting her nerves on fire. Of making her forget her sentence halfway through speaking. Of making her heart beat a little faster—okay, a lot faster.

The word *billionaire* lodged in her brain. He'd become the one thing he'd said he didn't want to be—a wealthy executive burning both ends of the candle. The

J.C. she had once fallen for had been determined to shake off his family expectations and become his own man, take his music on the road and go wherever the wind blew. To live the same devil-may-care life she wanted, city to city, no rules, no expectations, no roots holding them back. He couldn't be further from that right now if he tried. Seemed he'd not just stepped into the shoes his father had worn—but also had them custom-made.

If anything reminded her that J.C. was a mistake she didn't need to make, that was it.

Allie slapped the bill on the table, said something about coming back later, then headed off. J.C. returned to the table, paid the check and added a very generous tip. "Sorry about that. I keep getting interrupted."

"No problem." The need to leave, to get far away from J.C.—J.C. the *billionaire*—burned inside her. She gathered up her things and stuffed them in her purse. "We'll catch up later."

He hoisted Henry into his arms. With the sleeping child curled against his chest J.C. looked soft, vulnerable…yummy.

"Did you get all the answers you needed?"

"Yeah, I did." She tore her gaze away from the man she had once thought she knew as well as she knew herself. A man who had been transformed in the years since to a designer-shoe-wearing stranger. "I don't need to know anything else. The picture's crystal clear now."

She walked away, out into the cold winter air. It bit at her lungs, a quick dose of icy reality.

CHAPTER SIX

THE women clucked over him like he was a lost puppy. J.C. shifted in the chair at the coffee shop and wondered what insanity had made him agree to help Grace out with her grandmother's book club.

"We're so glad to have you here, J.C.," Mrs. Brimmel said. "It'll be nice to get the male perspective on Miss Austen."

Miss Watson shushed her. "Pauline, I doubt he read *Persuasion*. Let the poor man go. He'd be much more comfortable with a dartboard than with us old biddies."

He didn't tell her that he wasn't here for the ladies of the Beckett's Run Book Club. He was here for Grace, who had asked a favor of him with those big eyes and that teasing smile he'd never been able to resist.

"She's all wrong for you," his father had said over and over again. *"Flighty, irresponsible. She's going to run out of here one day and break your heart."*

She'd done exactly that, but he kept forgetting that when she smiled at him. She reminded him of the guitar in his closet, the music he used to love, the dreams he used to have. Then reality drew him back to the present, and to the responsibilities that weighed heavy on him.

J.C. had a thousand things on his to-do list, a cell phone that was about to self-combust with emails, texts and calls, all demanding his attention. Even though he knew Grace and he were as different as the proverbial tortoise and the hare, he stayed, watching Grace blush and stammer under the inquisitive glare of the Beckett's Run Book Club.

"Ladies, spending a morning in your company is never uncomfortable," J.C. said. That earned him more twittering from the book club and an eye-roll from Grace. "And I have read *Persuasion*. Several years ago, but I read it."

A collective gasp went up around the room. "You did?"

"You did?" Grace echoed. "Why on earth would you...? I mean, what made you want to?"

He shrugged. "I had a girlfriend in college who needed help with a paper on Austen. At the time I was trying to impress her, so I read the book."

"And how'd that work out?" Grace asked.

"The paper? Or the girlfriend?"

"Oh, the girlfriend, of course," Mrs. Brimmel said. The other book club ladies leaned in, rapt and eager.

"She got an A. And I believe she's now married to an English professor. I bet they talk about Austen every night."

The ladies laughed. J.C. cast a quick glance at Grace, who had a curious look on her face. It couldn't be jealousy, because the Grace he knew had never cared one bit about who he dated or what he did with his personal life. They had their summers, and in between she went off to her life and he went off to his. She'd arrive in town every June and school break, never asking what he'd been up to the months before, and they'd pick up as if they had never been apart.

"And what do you think about a lady's power of persuasion, J.C.?" Miss Watson asked.

"Oh, I think those are like super powers. A beautiful woman can talk a man into most anything."

"Even love?"

"Well, I wouldn't know about that. Seeing as how no one has managed to talk me into that yet." More laughter from the book club.

"You must be playing hard to get," Grace said. "Because, from what I hear, you're the most eligible bachelor this town has ever seen."

"I'm not *playing* hard to get, Grace." His gaze met hers. "At all."

She held his gaze for a long time, then looked away. "I'll let the single women in Beckett's Run know."

He grinned. "Alert the media?"

"I'll do even better than that. I'll send out an all-points bulletin."

"Hmm…that could be trouble," he said.

"Oh, everything about you is trouble, J.C. Carson."

At some point he'd forgotten the presence of the book club. His attention had honed in on Grace, on the way her lips moved when she talked, on that sassy little smile that accompanied every tease, on the way her ponytail danced along the back of her neck, like an invitation for his mouth to do the same.

"I think you're the one who's trouble, Grace McKinnon." Because right now he was having some very troubling thoughts. The kind that could make a man like him, a man who hadn't stepped off the prescribed path of his life in years, take a very serious detour.

"Well, that sounds like persuasion to me," Mrs. Brimmel said. The other ladies laughed, and the spell between J.C. and Grace was broken.

Grace picked up her copy of the novel—no more broken in today than the other day—and thumbed to a random page. "I wanted to get the group's thoughts on the events with Anne's cousin…uh…Mr.…Elliot. In chapter sixteen."

The group went on about their impressions of the book's theories on beauty and social standing, but J.C. wasn't listening. His gaze stayed on Grace, on that tempting flip of hair along her neck, and on the reasons why she seemed to dance closer to him, then jerk away.

Years ago, he'd thought he would marry Grace. Had planned to ask her in that foolish eighteen-year-old way that a boy had of thinking everything would be perfect if he just spent the rest of his days with the right girl. To J.C., Grace had been everything he hadn't been. Wild, adventurous, headstrong. She'd known what she wanted to do and be since she was old enough to hold a pencil, and nothing and no one would dissuade her. She'd ducked curfews and skirted rules, and encouraged him to do the same more than once. She'd turned down a soccer scholarship, opting instead to work her way through college at a school with a better journalism program. She'd started taking solo trips around the world the day she turned eighteen, just herself and a backpack and a pad of paper.

He was supposed to go on that first trip with her, using his guitar to make a living. Even had his bags packed. Then reality had hit, and he'd unpacked the bags, put the guitar in the closet, and gone back to following the path he'd been meant to take, the one he'd bucked until it became clear he could no longer afford that luxury. Grace had left town, without so much as a word, proving to him that her feelings for him were about as deep as a puddle.

A part of him wanted to ask why. Wanted to know how he could have been so wrong about her, so wrong about them. But he didn't. Because no matter what happened, he knew one thing for a fact—

He and Grace would never have that storybook ending, the kind created by Austen.

"Oh, my goodness, would you look at the time?" Mrs. Brimmel said. "We need to get to the Ladies' Tea at church." She turned to Grace. "Will you be with us next time, Grace? When we start *Little Women*? It's another love story, so maybe you might want to bring J.C. along, too." A devilish grin covered her face.

"I'll probably be gone by then," Grace said. "I'm only in town for the holidays."

"What a shame. Beckett's Run sure misses you." The other ladies concurred, dispensed hugs and warm wishes, then headed out of the coffee shop, bundled up like Eskimos.

J.C. checked his messages, read a text from the maintenance man he'd hired to set up several of the displays for the Winter Festival, then crossed to Grace. As much as he'd dreaded going to her grandmother's book club, he'd enjoyed the time away from the demands of the office. The fun of talking about something frivolous. It wasn't the kind of fun he'd had as a kid, but it was a nice departure from his day-to-day. And, most of all, he'd enjoyed seeing Grace. Especially when the ladies of Beckett's Run put her on the spot.

Damn. What was it about her that drew him even when he knew they were all wrong for each other? She was still the headstrong jackrabbit running for the door, and he was now the dependable tortoise, taking the safe and cautious path.

"I have to head over to the park to check on something," he said. "I don't know what you have going on right now, but maybe you want to go with me. You know, check out the inner workings of the festival and everything."

There. He'd clarified it. This wasn't a date, it was work.

"Sure. That sounds like fun."

He chuckled. "I'm just checking on some maintenance issues, so I can't guarantee fun."

"You know me, J.C." That smile winged its way across her face again. "I do guarantee fun."

"Oh, I remember that. Very well."

"Do you? Because it seems to me you're not the same guy I left behind. Now you're the guy with the emails and phone calls and button-down shirts." She skated a finger down the front of his shirt and searing heat raced through his veins.

For a moment he imagined her undoing those buttons, her gaze locked on his and that sexy, sassy smile on her lips. Her hands parting the panels of his shirt, then her skin against his, moving lower, lower—

"Now you're the guy with the emails and phone calls and button-down shirts."

She'd nailed him in a few words. The image constricted his throat, a noose constructed from responsibilities and expectations. Foolishness was what Grace represented. Not responsibility.

"Doesn't mean I'm not fun," he said, his voice quiet, dark.

"Oh, really?" She arched a brow. "So you're still the guy who would dive into a cold lake on the first day of March?"

"Yeah. I am." He wanted to be that guy still, Lord, how he wanted to be. He missed those days. He wanted to forget the ties and the emails and just be J.C., out on another adventure with Grace. Just one more fun time.

Her gaze met his, strong and sure. "Good." She slipped her arm into his and they headed out into the cold. "Then prove it to me."

Grace stood to the side, watching J.C. handle a flurry of issues and problems that could have pushed another man over the edge. Not only had the maintenance man come to him in a panic over a broken-down ride, but so too had two of the construction workers who were assembling the last parts of Santa's Village. J.C. solved each of their problems with fast efficiency and a couple of phone calls. All while his own phone buzzed and rang, a constant blur of activity. Throughout it all he kept his head and stayed focused, which kept those around him calm, too. He had a way of talking to people that calmed them down and got them refocused. Within minutes tempers cooled, and the festival got back on track.

"You handled that great. I'm impressed," she said when he joined her again.

"That was nothing. You should see some of the things I run into at work. Here, it's just a ride or a shed. At work, it's millions of dollars. But in the end the cost doesn't matter. If something is important to people, they want a solution. And I try to provide that."

"You're good at it."

"Thanks."

She leaned against the wall of the Mistletoe Wishes ride and studied him. "But you're not happy."

"Who says I'm not happy?"

"You do. It's in your eyes." She pushed off from the wall and came closer. "I have known you forever, J.C.

Carson, and I know when you're happy and when you're not."

Behind them, music began to play. Happy Christmas songs, a lyrical undertow to the ride. Red and white decorated boats sailed into a dark tunnel on a fake ice road constructed out of shimmery metal. Christmas lights twinkled inside the space, causing a soft glow to spill from the entrance.

"All set," called the maintenance man. "Should work like a dream now. You want to take a ride on it? Try her out?"

J.C. hesitated, his hand on his phone, his gaze going to the steady stream of emails pouring in. More demands for his time and attention. The J.C. he had become was rising to the surface again. She knew she shouldn't care, but she just couldn't—not right now, not for this moment—let him be that man. She may not love J.C. anymore, may not be part of his life now, but, damn it, she refused to let him become the very thing he'd despised.

His father.

John Carson had been a cold, distant man, who rarely cracked a smile and spent his days working, or talking about work. She'd never heard of him taking the family on vacation or going to J.C.'s basketball games or, heck, taking the kids to the park. J.C. had rarely talked about his father, and when he had, it was always around something to do with work. And most of all J.C.'s father had hated Grace and the "distractions" she caused his son. But John wasn't here right now, and J.C. looked like he could use a distraction.

"Anyway, I'll leave her running for a while," the maintenance man said. "Just flip this switch here if you want to try it out. Gotta go look at the lighting for

Santa's Village right now." He headed off to the other side of the park.

"What do you say?" Grace asked. "Want to take a spin?"

J.C. held up the phone. "I really should—"

"Have fun," she whispered, closing the gap by another foot. "Remember? You said you were going to prove it to me."

"Taking a ride is—"

"The first step." She grabbed his hand and pulled him into the tunnel. "So let's do it."

"Grace, I shouldn't—"

"Argue with me. You know I always win." She laughed, then tugged him deeper into the dark space. The boats circled around the track, passing by the boarding dock and into the ebony recesses. She leaned over, flipped the switch, and the next boat chugged to a stop. "Get in, J.C., and let's see how fast we can make this thing go."

He chuckled. "It's set to one speed and one speed only. There's no racing in the tunnel of love. It's meant to go slow and easy." He glanced at her, his blue eyes holding the glint of a tease. "Are you up for that?"

"I'm up for anything," Grace said, and climbed into the boat. But as J.C. sat in the space beside her she realized how confining the small vessel was, how it was meant to bring two lovers close together, to encourage them to embrace. A tunnel of love—the kind of place that meant kissing, touching…falling.

Before she could change her mind the boat jerked to a start and headed down the mechanical path. The movement brought her against J.C. He draped his arm over the back of the seat. "Not much room in here."

"Not much at all. Kind of reminds me of—"

"The Ferris wheel at the summer fair," he said, at the same time she did.

Grace laughed. "That thing was tiny. I don't even know how it called itself a Ferris wheel."

"The whole fair was tiny. But it was fun."

Her gaze met his. In the dark, all she could see was the glimmering reflection of the Christmas lights, dancing in the pools of his eyes. "It was."

"We used to have a lot of fun, Grace."

"We did."

"I miss those days."

"Me, too, J.C." She thought of the trips she'd taken, the destinations she'd stayed in over the course of her career. She'd been all over the world, and nowhere had she laughed as much or enjoyed herself as much as she had during those summers with J.C. Carson.

Letting herself get swept up again, though, would be a foolish mistake. She wasn't staying and she shouldn't act like a woman who was.

J.C. shifted, which brought his leg against hers. Heat raced along her skin and made her pulse thunder. She glanced down at his arm, his thigh, and the urge to touch him became her only thought.

Oh, this was trouble. Big, big trouble. She jerked away and reached for the side of the boat. "Come on, let's check this thing out." Before he could stop her, she leapt out of the boat and onto the platform running alongside them.

"Hey, we're not supposed to be up there."

"You're the boss, J.C. You can do anything you want. Come on—find me." She dashed off into the pretend night, ducking behind one of the dozens of Christmas trees lining the side. Grace crouched down, hiding her body amongst the wide branches of a fake fir.

"This is nuts," he said, but a laugh escaped him anyway.

She heard the sound of his footsteps on the platform, hard at first, then softer, as he snuck among the trees. She shifted to circle to the other side of the fir as J.C. came around to the back. Her foot caught on a tree base, and the fir wobbled, threatening to fall. She caught it, but not before she heard J.C. say, "Got you!"

Grace scrambled to her feet and ran off, laughing as she wove in and out of the trees. The blinking lights cast a golden blanket over the space, illuminating J.C. as he emerged from the faux forest, still laughing. "Give up yet?" she called out.

"Never."

She laughed again, then charged down the back wall. Around them, the Christmas music kept on playing, and the boats kept on moving. The world of Beckett's Run had ceased to exist inside the dark tunnel of the Mistletoe Wishes ride, and a part of Grace wished she could stay here forever, that she could forget the job and family and life waiting for her outside these walls.

She heard a rustle, and before she could move J.C.'s hand curled around her arm. "Got you. And this time I'm not letting go."

"You promise?" She said the words as a joke, but the other Grace, the one who had once believed she and J.C. would be together forever, held her breath and waited for his answer.

"That might not be too practical," he said with a laugh.

"And you are the sensible one." She forced a smile against her disappointment.

"I wasn't always," he said. "Especially when it came to you."

Her breath lodged in her throat again. She wanted to ask what he meant, wanted to know whether he meant that as a good thing or a bad thing, but she couldn't bear to hear the answer. All she wanted right now was this moment, this tiny world of just her and J.C.

And, God help her, she wanted him, too. She always had.

"Oh, Grace," he said, his voice as dark as the tunnel around them, and in those two words she heard the same desire, the same want that pulsed inside her chest. She waited a fraction of a second and then, finally, J.C. did what she had wanted him to do since she'd crashed her car into that snow bank.

He leaned in and kissed her, capturing her mouth with his in a heated electric rush, one made sweeter and hotter by the passing of time, the knowledge of a past lover. Sparks arced in her body, erupted in her brain, overrode her common sense. J.C. captured her face with his hands, a sweet, gentle move that countered the hot demands of his kiss. He made her feel treasured and sexy, all at the same time, and all she wanted right now was more of that.

She leaned into him. Beside them, the boats jerked along on their lazy ride, bumping softly in the quiet, but she didn't care. Her arms circled his back and she pressed him into her, until not a breath of space remained between them. He groaned, and his tongue darted into her mouth, setting off another fire deep in her belly. Her hands went to his hair, burying deep in those dark locks, wanting…

More. Wanting him.

She'd never forgotten what it was like to be touched by J.C. Carson. To be loved by him, to have him take his sweet, slow time kissing her body, touching her skin, igniting her passion. They had learned together, really, the two of them starting out as fumbling teen-agers, then daring more and more with each summer, until one summer—

She jerked back so fast she nearly brought the en-tire row of trees down with her. What was she doing? Going back to those days? Hadn't she learned her lesson before? She and J.C. were no good together, and never would be. Kissing him only made that reality hurt more.

"We can't...we can't do that." Her breath heaved out of her chest, and her body cried foul.

"And what do you think we're doing?"

"Opening a door we shut a long time ago." She turned toward the ride, stepped into the nearest boat, and reached for the handle to the dock on the other side. J.C. followed, reaching for her arm.

"You're running again, Grace."

"I'm not." She'd never run from him. That was what he didn't understand. She'd only done what he had told her to do all those years ago—she'd left without him. His father had said J.C. would be happier, and she would be, too. She told herself he'd been right. "I'm just not... staying."

"That's the same thing."

She pivoted back to him as the hurt she'd felt that day years and years ago surged to the surface. *We had plans,* she wanted to scream at him. *You were supposed to be there forever. To be the one I could depend on. Always. And you let me down.* "You would know, J.C."

Then she headed out of the tunnel, and back into the cold winter sunshine.

CHAPTER SEVEN

J.C. WALKED through the door of his mother's house, hoping this time would be different. But no smells of dinner cooking greeted him. No scent of pine cleanser stung his nose. There was only the same scene as the day before and all the days before that—the soft undertow of the television playing yet another sappy movie that had gone direct to video. On the living room floor, Henry played with a set of toy blocks, building something that could have been a house, a castle or a gorilla enclosure.

Henry scrambled to his feet and plowed into J.C. "Uncle Jace! Look what I made!"

J.C. followed his nephew into the living room and marveled over the bright creation. "That's a great... house," he said.

"It's not a house. It's a rocket!" Henry jerked up the tower and started running around the room, making *vroom-vroom* sounds.

"Henry, please keep it down. Grandma is trying to watch her show."

His mother had never even taken her eyes off the television when she spoke. Henry nodded, then sat on the carpet and went back to building. J.C. crossed to the seat in front of his mother.

Grace's words from earlier came back to him. She'd

accused him of never having any fun, and she was right. But what she didn't understand was the enormous pressure and responsibility that lay on J.C.'s shoulders. First the business, then his widowed mother, and now his orphaned nephew. There were days when J.C. felt like he might bow to the weight of all that, but he knew he couldn't. Because if he did, people would get hurt. He was the rock they all stood upon, and a rock never crumbled.

Then what was that in the tunnel today? his mind asked.

A moment of insanity. He'd let himself get swept up in the game and lost track of the end result. For a moment he'd been eighteen again, Grace hot and soft in his arms, the world some far off thing.

Then she'd broken away and done what Grace always did—left.

Which was exactly what Grace was going to do after Christmas, too. Right now J.C. needed stability and predictability in his life—*that* was who he was, what people needed him to be. Grace was as far from those adjectives as she was from the moon.

He turned his attention back to his mother. "Hey, Mom, what's for dinner?"

"Sandwiches."

"I'm going to have to get that printed on the menu here, we have it so often." J.C. gave her a grin. "Come on, Mom, let's go make something. You love to cook."

"I used to. Not now." She thumbed the volume on the remote.

J.C. got to his feet, and started for the door, to do what he had done for weeks now—let it go and put off the hard discussions for another day. Then he glanced at his nephew and knew it could wait no longer. The holidays were here, and soon J.C. had to make a decision about staying in Beckett's Run or going back to Boston.

J.C. worried that if he returned to Boston his grieving mother would withdraw even further, which would hurt Henry. J.C. pivoted back. "Henry, can you do me a favor? Can you go in your room and draw a picture of a horse for Grace? She'd really like that."

"Yup! I'll draw the horsey from the zoo. Grace is scared of him too cuz he sneezes funny." Henry dashed off, enthused and excited.

When he was gone, J.C. stood in front of the television. His mother let out a sigh of exasperation. "Mom, we need to talk."

"I'm watching my show."

"You're always watching your show. I think you should watch your grandson." Before her daughter's death Anne Carson had been an engaged grandmother, who saw Henry daily and took him to the park and the playground. Since her daughter's fatal car accident Anne had barely acknowledged Henry.

"He's fine."

"He's not," J.C. countered. "He wants a grandmother who interacts with him. He wants something other than sandwiches for dinner. He wants you to look at his rocket and tell him it's the best rocket you've ever seen." Things his mother used to do with J.C. when he was little. She'd been the one who had encouraged him, paid for his music lessons out of her pin money. She'd been the one who had dipped Easter eggs with J.C. and his sister, who had camped out in the living room on summer afternoons. Before J.C.'s sister died, his mother had been the one who kept the family together. Now it seemed all she did was fall apart a little more each day.

"I do that for Henry." She tried to peer around J.C. but he remained where he was.

"No, you don't. You know it, and I know it, and poor Henry does, too. He needs you, Mom. Just like…" J.C. swallowed hard, then went on, "I used to when I was his age."

All those unspoken memories hung in the air. The tough, demanding, cold father, tempered by Anne's warm heart, tender touches. J.C. often wondered how he and his sister would have turned out if they hadn't had their mother to ease their difficult childhoods. He knew Anne had loved John, loved him with a fierceness that J.C. envied. The few times J.C. had seen his father vulnerable had been with his wife, as if she was the only one he could let down his guard around.

It took a moment, but his mother finally raised her gaze to his. "I'm trying, J.C. I really am."

"I know you are, but you're not helping yourself or him by watching these shows every day. It's Christmas, Mom. Your favorite time of year and you haven't even wanted to put up the tree yet."

"It's a lot of work and—"

"And that's an excuse. I told you I'd help. Hell, I'll do the whole thing if you want."

"I'm just not in the mood for the holiday." Her gaze went to the far wall, past him, into moments that had come and gone long ago. When she didn't say anything J.C. shifted away from the television with a sigh. He'd tried.

"Don't worry about it," he said. "I'll do it this week-end."

This was what Grace didn't know, or see, or understand, when she pushed him to be that wild kid he'd once been. That kid had grown up and had people who would fall apart if he didn't keep it together.

J.C.'s mother got to her feet and stood before him. "You're always taking care of me. It should be the other way around."

"I don't mind. Think of it as payback for doing my laundry when I was younger."

That brought a spark of life to his mother's eyes, and for the first time in a while J.C. began to hope that things would change. "And you had a lot of laundry for one little boy."

He shrugged. "Being a boy is a messy business."

She glanced at the space where Henry had been just a while earlier. "I see a lot of you in him. The way he looks at the world, the way he loves to create, to build. He's a bit impetuous, too, like you used to be."

J.C. didn't think about his creative, impetuous sides. One of these days Henry would grow up too and those things would be pushed to the side. The thought saddened J.C.

"Henry's a good kid." Already J.C. had gotten used to seeing his nephew every day. He hated the thought of moving back to Boston. He'd asked his mother several times about moving into his Boston house, but she'd refused. She loved Beckett's Run, always had, and didn't want to leave.

"He is a good kid. And…he deserves more than this. You're right, J.C." His mother nodded, and in that gesture, J.C. saw her turn a corner, one that took her a step away from her grief. "Maybe we can string some lights or something this week."

"That would be great." It was a start, and for J.C. that was enough. He took his mother's hand and met her eyes. "If it wasn't for you, Mom, we wouldn't have had a Christmas. You made this house a home, even on the days when it felt like…" He let his voice trail off instead of saying the words.

"A prison?" she supplied. Anne's features softened. She cupped his jaw. "Your father was a hard man. I'm sorry for that."

J.C. didn't want to talk about his father, who had passed away four years ago. That was a past he had put behind him, a past he intended to keep there. Choices had been made, paths had been taken that couldn't be undone now.

He thought of that kiss he'd shared with Grace, and wondered for the first time in a long while where he would be if he and Grace had worked out. If they had done what they'd planned and run off into the sunset, him with his guitar, her with her pen. Would they still be happy all these years later? Or would they have learned a life without expectations was as empty as a bag of air?

It didn't matter. Then, and now, J.C. couldn't afford to take off on a whim. That weight sat heavy on J.C.'s shoulders, even as he wanted to delay Henry's leap into being a grown-up as long as possible. Maybe find a way to bring out the kid in Henry, and in the process find a bit of the kid in himself, without forgetting the main task—to take care of his family.

"Don't apologize, Mom. We did okay. And now we have a chance to do even better for Henry. We're all he's got, and he deserves the best Christmas ever."

Tears shimmered in Anne's eyes. She nodded. "You're right." Then she covered his hand with her own. "The tree's in the attic. Why don't you go bring it down? And I'll start dinner."

* * *

Grace had spent the better part of the night tossing and turning, wondering about J.C. and then cursing herself for caring. So he was taking care of his sister's son. So he seemed…different. So he had kissed her.

And her body had responded the same as always, with fire.

Didn't mean she was going to open that door again. She was here to get a story, restore her career and get the hell out of Beckett's Run. Hopefully without running into any other members of her family.

Gram had gone to church, leaving Grace a note on the kitchen table beside a basket of blueberry muffins. Grace slathered butter on one, popped a big bite in her mouth, then ran down her notes from the day before. She tapped her pencil against the pad.

Nothing she had so far contained that hook she needed. That unique spin. Everything about the Beckett's Run Winter Festival in her notes fit the definition of cliché. Small-town Christmas celebration, lots of mistletoe and greenery, a great tourist stop for a family to while away a weekend. She'd done a hundred stories like this, and for years that had been the foundation she built her career upon. But that wasn't the kind of story that was going to bring her career back from the dead. Or get her editor to give her a second chance.

She needed something more. Something like…

I want to give that Christmas experience to the people of Beckett's Run, and to those on the outside looking in, to help them believe in magic again.

She stared at J.C.'s words, then thought of him with his nephew. People believing in magic. People like Henry.

Henry, a vulnerable, hopeful little boy, with big blue eyes and a trembling smile, who had lost both his parents at a time of year meant for families and hope. The kind of story people connected with, remembered.

A quiver of hesitation ran through her. This was J.C's nephew. Someone who was practically family. The last thing J.C. wanted, she was sure, was to have his personal life in the media.

She thought again of her editor's words. *Washed-up. Lost your touch.*

Maybe she had stumbled, but she hadn't lost it entirely. She still knew a good story when she saw one, and this was a good story. She could already see how she would shift the coverage of the Winter Festival to what came from a child's eye level. It would be whimsical and bittersweet, the kind of article people shared with their friends. The kind of article that careers—or renewed careers—were built upon. Surely J.C. would see that—and trust her to write a heartwarming, nonexploitative piece.

"You need to put your heart into your stories. Then the reader will laugh and cry right along with you."

That was what this story would be. She knew it, deep in her gut. Steve had told her to show that she cared in her writing, and she realized that after just a couple days she did care about Henry, and that fueled her to want to do a good job with his story.

She had her story. Now to make J.C. agree.

Grace ran upstairs, showered and changed into jeans and a V-neck white tee, then pulled on a thick green sweater. She swiped on a minimum of make-up, swung her hair into a ponytail, then tugged on some boots and headed out the door. She cursed herself for not getting J.C.'s phone number but figured in a town as small as Beckett's Run he wouldn't be that hard to find. She could have called his mother's house, but knowing J.C.

he was undoubtedly out and about, working on another task for the Winter Festival.

Her car fishtailed on the slick roads as she turned onto Main. She slowed, pulling into the parking lot of the drugstore. Rick Anderson, the pharmacist, had lived in town longer than anyone, and knew more about the goings-on than a high-tech satellite. If anyone knew where to find J.C., it was Rick.

But that wasn't who she encountered when she stepped through the glass doors. Grace drew up short when she saw a familiar figure with short blonde hair standing by the Christmas candy display. She blinked. Was she seeing things? "Mom? What are you doing here?"

Lydia McKinnon—though she hadn't been a McKinnon for many years—reached forward and drew her youngest daughter into a hug. The scent of her perfume and fresh snow filled Grace's nostrils. The hug comforted and suffocated all at the same time. "Oh, my God, Grace! Mary said you were in town."

Grace drew back. "Gram? When did you talk to her?"

"This morning. I called her when I was almost to town. She invited me for dinner tomorrow night so we could catch up." Her mother hugged her again. "Oh, I'm so excited to see you!"

Gram, always trying to create a happy ending in a family that had never been anything close to happy. Grace stepped out of the embrace before she got too used to it. Chances were, her mother was on her way *through* town, and on to something else, and would be gone before the table was set. "I didn't know you were coming to town."

"Well, neither did I, but then I was talking to Hope and Faith—"

"You talked to them? When?"

"I've always talked to them, and I would talk to you all the time, too, if anyone could pin you down, you globetrotter." Lydia smiled. "Anyway, the other day your sisters and I were talking about all the wonderful things happening in their lives, and I just wanted to come here and see them and have a perfect family holiday."

Wonderful things happening in Hope and Faith's lives? Hurt bloomed in Grace's chest. Her sisters hadn't called her and told her a thing. Had the three McKinnon girls really drifted that far apart that good news couldn't be shared?

Or had Grace been the one to pull back? Over the years her sisters had called and emailed and texted, but Grace, always busy with the next assignment, another plane to catch, had vowed to catch up later. Later had never come.

"The girls are on their way into town," her mother went on, "and should be here before Christmas Day." Lydia clasped her hands together. "I'm so excited to have us all together again. I have so many plans, Grace. It's going to be an amazing holiday."

"That's great, Mom," Grace said. She didn't add that she knew her mother well and doubted Lydia would hang around town long enough for the holiday to arrive. There'd be another man, another adventure, something to drag Lydia away—or rather something that Lydia allowed to drag her away from her family. There'd be no amazing holiday. Just another disappointment to add to the list.

"Listen, let's get a bite to eat. I haven't seen you in forever." Lydia smiled. "So let's get some lunch and catch up."

"I can't. I have things to do today. But maybe later."

Lydia's face fell, and for a moment Grace wanted to apologize, to say *Yes, sure, let's get burgers and act like nothing ever changed.* But she didn't.

"Okay. You have my cell, right?"

"Yeah. I'll call. I promise." Grace gave her mother a fast hug, then turned and exited the drugstore. It wasn't until she got back to her car that she'd realized that she'd left without the one thing she needed—information.

She sat in her car and let out a long sigh. What was it about seeing her mother that set her on edge? Five seconds into seeing her and Grace wanted to run for the hills. She tugged out her cell, scrolled through the contacts, then paused, her finger over the name. Finally, she pressed the button and waited for the call to go through.

"You've reached Hope McKinnon." Hope's voice exploded in a breathless rush in her voicemail message. "I can't come to the phone right now, because I'm..." a giggle—from *Hope*, of all people—then another rush of breath "...busy, but I promise to return your call soon."

The excitement and happiness in Hope's words drew Grace up short. The last time they'd talked they'd been fighting about Hope helping Grace out with an article. The nightmarish Fiji article, the one from where it had all gone so far downhill that now her editor had sent her on a required vacation, or rather a forced leave of absence. Now Hope sounded as joyous as a kid at an amusement park.

"Hey, it's Grace. Gram said you were coming to Beckett's Run and I wanted to give you a heads-up, in case she didn't already tell you. Mom's here. For as long as Mom will stay. Maybe she'll be gone by the time you arrive, or maybe she'll stay. Who knows with her? Anyway....I just wanted to let you know."

Grace hung up the phone and put it back in her

pocket. She thought of calling Faith, then stopped. She didn't need her sisters to reinforce what she already knew—that having their mother here wouldn't end well. It never did, and Grace wasn't about to get her hopes up now.

Instead she put the car in gear and headed down the street. She didn't know where she was going to stop until she made the last turn and ended up parked alongside the town park. She turned off the car and got out, slipping on her gloves as a gust of winter's chill raced down her spine.

The festival preparations were nearly done, from what she could see. The entire Beckett's Run park had been decorated in red, green and white. Pine swags looped between oversized wreaths hanging on the streetlights, while a mini Christmas village anchored the center of the park. To the right, the pond had been changed into an ice skating rink, where dozens of people circled, their breath forming frosty clouds. Santa's Village dominated the eastern side of the park, complete with a mini-toy factory and a place for the big guy to take appointments and hear Christmas wishes. Reindeer pranced inside a wooden pen located beside a smaller green building labeled "Elf Shop."

"Too much?"

Grace whirled around at the sound of J.C.'s deep voice behind her. When she saw him her heart stuttered, and her mind flashed back to that hot kiss in the dark tunnel of the Mistletoe Wishes ride. An apt name, if people only knew. Damn, that man could kiss. And damn her hormones for wanting him to do it again. Right here. Right now.

"It's Christmas. There's no such thing as too much, if you ask my grandmother."

He chuckled. "Wait till you see the swimming swans and leaping lords we booked."

"You didn't?"

"No, but I have to admit I considered it."

She chuckled. "You always did like to do things in a huge, memorable way, J.C."

"Not me."

"Oh, really?" She leaned back against a tree and crossed her arms over her chest. "Remember the town picnic? When you sang 'Happy Birthday' to me from the roof of the gazebo?"

"That was…an anomaly."

"And the time you caught the biggest fish in the annual fish derby?"

"Beginner's luck."

"Maybe, but no one else tossed their fish back and dove in after it."

"It was a hot day."

She shook her head. "I don't get you. You used to be so…spontaneous, J.C. Now you're all serious and grown-up. It's as if that person you used to be never existed."

"That's the key, Grace. I grew up."

He took a step closer, winnowing the space between them to mere inches. The winter cold disappeared, replaced by a heat that raced through her veins, sped up her heart.

"We both did."

She laughed and looked away. She wouldn't call herself a grown-up—at least not entirely grown-up. "I don't know about that."

He put a finger under her jaw and turned her face until she was looking at him again. He had the bluest eyes. The kind of eyes that stayed in a girl's memory…

forever. She'd never forgotten him, no matter how many times she told herself otherwise. J.C. Carson had always lingered in the back of her memory, a shadow she couldn't shake. Not that she'd tried very hard.

Maybe it was because he was her first—first everything. First real friend, first boyfriend, first lover. Hadn't she read once that a girl always compared every man in her life to her first? That was all it was. Not that J.C. had been special or amazing or anything like that.

Because he'd also been her first heartbreak.

She needed to remember that more than anything else.

"You are very, very grown-up, Grace." His thumb traced her lower lip, slow, easy.

Okay, remembering that last fact was a little harder than she thought. She took in a sharp breath, her gaze locked on his. She knew she should step away. Should stop this before it went...wherever it might go. But she didn't. Because the part that remembered all those other firsts kept winning out. "It's all an act."

"No, it's not." His gaze dropped to her lips. "You may fool others, but I know you."

"And what do you know?"

"That we keep dancing around this subject."

"What subject?"

"This one." He leaned in and kissed her again, this time slower, sweeter. Her resistance faded in the wake of his tender touch, and she leaned into him, her hands going to his hair, pulling him closer. It was wonderful and amazing and as memorable as their first kiss.

No, it was better. After that kiss in the tunnel and this one now she had stopped telling herself that her memories were flawed, that she had built up J.C. in her mind to be a better lover than he'd been in reality.

Because he was amazing, in person and in memory. J.C. was everything she'd remembered—and more. He touched her exactly the way she liked to be touched. Kissed her exactly the way she liked to be kissed. It was as if he had opened the book of Grace and memorized every page.

She knew, oh, she knew, that he was an incredible, tender, giving lover who could send her soaring and bring her back to earth with a gentle touch, a whisper in her ear. And she wanted, oh, how she wanted to take him to her bed.

That was the whole problem. What she wanted and what she knew she should do.

She jerked away from him and her hormones screamed in protest. "We keep doing this. And we can't. Going back to where we were before. That would be a mistake." She inhaled, held the breath, then let it out in one long, slow exhale, letting sanity replace the desire. "A huge mistake."

"A mistake we've made before." His gaze sought hers, then he nodded, and the serious, grown-up J.C. returned. "But you're right."

"Good. I'm glad you agree." Though being right didn't have the satisfaction she'd expected. She ignored the disappointment in her chest and took a step back. "So, let's concentrate on why we're really here. The festival." She reached into her inside pocket and withdrew her notebook and pen. "I wanted to talk to you some more about it."

If the new direction in their relationship bothered him, J.C. didn't show it. Part of Grace hated that about J.C. How he could throw up a wall and keep part of himself hidden from her. There'd been a time when she'd thought she knew everything there was to know about J.C.

She'd been wrong.

These last few days had proved that. Every time she thought she saw the old J.C., the one she had first met in that diner over a chicken pot pie, this other one, the one he'd vowed he'd never be, rose to the surface. If she was smart she'd stop trying to figure out why and concentrate on her career.

"You know, I don't feel like talking about work right now. In fact, I don't feel like working at all. I'm ready to have some fun," he said, and the serious J.C. disappeared. His grin quirked up on one side in the way she remembered, the way it had the day they had run through the high school, the day he'd jumped in that icy pond. "Meet me back here in an hour. And wear some snow pants."

CHAPTER EIGHT

HENRY stood at the top of the hill, bundled up like a giant marshmallow. His snowsuit covered him from head to toe, and every time he moved he had the jerky movements of a robot, not a little boy. But happiness radiated from his features, and laughter spilled from him in a steady stream.

And J.C. felt like he could breathe for the first time in a month.

His mother wasn't a hundred percent involved with Henry yet, but she had made the first attempts at setting up for the holiday season, and when J.C. had left today there'd been a roast in the slow cooker. One step at a time, he told himself, and it would all be okay. Henry's mood was brighter, his smile bigger. He had that magic look in his eyes, the one that radiated from children at Christmas. The very look J.C. had worked so hard and so long to bring to his nephew.

Grace made her way up the snowy hill, looking both sexy and practical in a thick blue winter coat and matching snow pants. The boots she wore—zebra patterns that came nearly to her knee and had a thick faux-fur top—were all Grace. Quirky, yet fun.

"Sledding? *That's* what you want me to do?"

"Yep."

She cast a dubious glance at the long wooden sled in J.C.'s hands. "Well, if I'm going, you're going."

"I'm no good at sledding. Not exactly my area of expertise."

"One little accident, J.C. And it was years ago. I'm sure you've improved your driving abilities since then."

Henry tugged on J.C.'s sleeve. "Are we gonna go, Uncle Jace?"

J.C. had invited Grace along so that she would do this, and he could get back to work. Maybe make a few phone calls while Grace and Henry rode the slopes. He hadn't expected to be part of it himself. As much as he wanted to, he had details of a merger breathing down his neck, with lawyers, accountants and other suits all waiting on his responses. Carson Investments needed some attention, too, even as the snowy hill and Henry's big blue eyes beckoned. He didn't have time for fun or sledding or anything but work. "Sorry, buddy, no can do. Grace is going to take you down the hill."

Henry pouted. "I want you to go, too."

"That's two votes for J.C. to go," Grace said, then waved at the sled. "You're not chickening out, are you?"

The challenge in her voice awakened something inside him. Something he hadn't listened to in a long, long time. Something that reminded him of who he'd used to be...before.

Before the emails and board meetings, the to-do lists and the power suits. He could take one ride, and just for a minute forget all those things. The part of him that had pretended for a little while on those hot summer days that his father wasn't waiting at home with lists and chores and extra homework for J.C. to do. For those moments J.C. could just...*be*. The urge to do that called like music, rising in his chest.

The snow began to fall around him, light flakes kissing against his coat, his face. *Just...be,* it seemed to whisper. *Just...be.*

"Okay, let's do this." J.C. grinned, then brought the toboggan to the top of the hill, cemented himself on the front, then turned to Henry. "Climb on, buddy."

Henry clambered onto the sled and put his arms around his uncle's waist, sure, trusting. J.C. looked back at Grace. "And now you, milady."

She laughed, and when her gaze met his he knew she was thinking of another winter, another sledding trip. She'd been sixteen, visiting over Christmas break. Their first kiss had been shared on this very hill, after they'd skidded off the path and into a snow bank, ending up in a tangle of arms and legs. He'd looked at her and for the first time really seen her, as a woman, not as a girl or a friend.

And from that moment on things had never been the same.

"Are you sure I can trust your steering? Last time we did this I ended up buried under the snow and…" she lowered her voice "…you."

"I remember." Every single second.

"Me, too." She smiled, a soft, secret smile that seemed meant only for him.

Henry looked from one to the other. "Are we gonna go?"

J.C. chuckled and ruffled the boy's hair. "Yep. Right now." Then he looked at Grace. "Are you ready?"

"As ready as I'll ever be."

"Trust me, Grace," he said, and wondered if he was still talking about downhill rides. She climbed on behind Henry, propping her legs onto J.C.'s, forming a human sandwich of protection for the little boy. J.C.

looked down at those zebra boots draped over his thighs, making his thoughts veer for a moment from blankets of snow to blankets on a bed, then he drew himself back to the present, took the controls of the sled, shouted back a quick "Let's go!" then pushed off.

The sled rushed down the hill, past the families tromping back up, past the thick green pine trees that fronted the woods on one side of the park. Cold air frosted J.C.'s face, burned in his lungs. He hunkered down, using the controls to keep the toboggan heading for the soft flat space at the base of the hill. And then, just as fast as it began, the ride was over and the sled was sliding to a stop.

Henry clambered off. "That was fun! I want to do it again!"

His nephew was right. The whole ride had been fun. A break from the demands and expectations of his life. Inside his pocket his cell phone buzzed with a missed call. J.C.'s hand went to the cell, then he stopped and let the call go to voicemail. A flicker of guilt, but he ignored it. He could take this time and the world would not stop spinning.

"You got it, Henry." J.C. got to his feet, then put out a hand to help Grace rise. But she had already stood, and didn't need his help. "You want to go again?"

"When have I ever said no to a fast ride?" She laughed and he realized how much he had missed that sound. "And thanks for not hitting that snow bank."

"I told you to trust me."

"I know. And you know how good I am at trusting people." Her eyes danced with merriment.

"Oh, I know." His gaze met hers, then he turned away and bent down to his nephew. "Want a ride on my shoulders, little guy?"

"Sure!" Henry put out his arms and J.C. hoisted him up. Grace grabbed the sled and the three of them made their way back up the hill, looking for all appearances like any other family in the Beckett's Run park. At the top, J.C. lowered Henry to the ground, then let out a breath.

"I've been spending too much time behind a desk." He stretched out the kinks in his back. Like a reminder his phone began to ring again, and the guilt rang louder in his head.

Grace pressed a hand to his before he could answer the call. "Let's race," Grace whispered in his ear. "And for just a second pretend we have wings."

Just for a second. He muted the phone, then bent down, set the sled in place and repeated the actions of earlier, climbing on the front, then waiting for Henry to settle his small frame in the middle. Grace got on the back again, and those damned zebra boots reappeared on his thighs, like a visual representation of her challenge to race.

He shoved off, and as they rushed down the hill a second time he thought how right she was. How, for the few seconds it took to go from the top to the bottom, it seemed as if they *had* taken flight. Behind him, Henry laughed and squeezed J.C.'s waist tight. Grace's legs pressed against his thighs. Too soon, the sled came to a stop and they climbed off. A flush filled Grace's cheeks, brightened her eyes.

When he'd asked for her help he'd thought it would be a good idea. A way to help Henry deal with his grief and find the spirit of Christmas again. After all, J.C. wouldn't be called the fun one in the family, at least not anymore, and his grieving mother had trouble finding ways to keep her rambunctious grandchild busy.

Of everyone he knew, Grace was the one person who embodied fun. She reminded him of who he'd used to be—before his life had changed.

Except being with her kept opening those doors he'd done a good job shutting a long time ago. The things that had broken them apart still existed, and no amount of sledding or laughter could leap that fence.

"Again?" Henry asked.

J.C.'s phone buzzed. Persistent, demanding, and angry about being ignored earlier. He fished it out of his pocket, and glanced at the Caller ID. His C.O.O., Charles, who had already left three voicemails. He couldn't put this off forever. That was the trouble with reality—it inserted itself at the worst possible time. "How about you go with Grace?"

"Okay." Henry slipped his little hand into Grace's. "Are you a good driver?"

Grace bent down to his level. "The best. You ready?"

Henry nodded, and the two of them climbed on the sled and took off. J.C. answered the call, but his gaze and attention stayed on Grace and Henry. On the way they laughed as they careened down the hill, on the happiness on Henry's face and on the way he hung tight to Grace, then jumped up and down with excitement when the sled came to a stop.

"J.C.? You listening?"

"Oh, yeah." Then he realized he hadn't heard a word his C.O.O. had said. He turned away from the sledding hill and faced the pond instead, filled with ice skaters circling the frozen water. "What did you say again?"

On the other end of the phone, Charles went on about the state of the company's finances. He reviewed the information about the upcoming acquisition, something that J.C. had been excited about—

Before.

Before he'd moved back to Beckett's Run. Before he'd stepped in as a surrogate parent to Henry. Before Grace McKinnon came back into his life.

"Let me call you back later. Email me the numbers and I'll take a look at them."

"But—"

"I'll call you. Don't worry so much." J.C. said goodbye, then hung up the phone. Before he even tucked the cell back in his pocket it started ringing again. By the time he finished the conversation with his accountant, his lawyer was beeping in. Grace and Henry had reached the top of the hill and taken one more ride to the bottom before J.C. disentangled himself from his phone. A half dozen voicemails still waited for him, and emails flooded his phone's inbox in a steady stream.

"Uncle Jace, are you coming?" Henry asked. "Grace's gonna drive again! She goes really fast!"

J.C. arched a brow in Grace's direction.

"Not too fast," Grace said. "Come on, Mr. Overachiever. Play hooky with us a while longer."

"I can't." He thought of all the messages he'd ignored this afternoon already. He couldn't keep letting his business flounder without him. He had a responsibility, and ignoring it wouldn't make it disappear. He hated that he was going to have to disappoint his nephew. "Henry, we need to go home now."

Henry's face fell, and the happiness that had radiated from him just a second ago evaporated. "Okay."

No argument. No begging to stay. Nothing but a solemn agreement. That broke J.C.'s heart. Stoic Henry, trying so hard to be good.

"If it's okay with you," Grace said, "I'll stay here

with Henry awhile longer, then meet you back at your mom's house."

"Are you sure?"

"Yup." She glanced down at Henry. "We're getting along okay, aren't we, kid?"

Henry nodded. "Uh-huh. Grace isn't a stranger, Uncle Jace. She's my friend, too."

J.C. chuckled. "I think you're right, buddy."

Grace offering to take Henry was something J.C. would never have expected to hear. Grace had surprised him—a lot—in the last few days. Still, he hesitated. "How are you going to get over to my mom's? It's too far to walk. And you'll never fit the sled in that clown car of yours."

"We'll be fine, J.C.," Grace said.

"Please, Uncle Jace?"

He glanced down at Henry, big blue eyes filled with tentative hope. J.C. let out a sigh. Two against one. "Okay, you guys stay, but take my truck instead and I'll drive your car."

"You. Drive my sportscar."

"I can handle a sportscar."

"Oh, I know you can. In the past. I just wondered if you remembered how to drive one," she teased.

He remembered. Too well. The tiny little sportscar he'd borrowed from his cousin Mike, hoping to impress Grace on their first "real" date. They'd hung out a thousand times over those summers she spent at her grandmother's house, but after that kiss in the snow when they'd been teenagers the easy friendship they'd had became layered with a new kind of tension, an attack of nerves every time he got within ten feet of her. He'd borrowed the car, and picked her up at Mary's house, then headed for Carol's. "I was a cautious driver."

"If you'd gone any slower they would have arrested you for blocking traffic." She grinned. "I thought it was…cute."

"Cute?" He arched a brow. "You know guys hate to be called *cute*."

"Yeah, I know." The smile that crossed her face held a sassy edge. "And it was cute. Very. Cute."

He chuckled. "You are a stubborn woman, Grace McKinnon."

Her features sobered and her eyes met his. "Some people say stubbornness is a plus, not a minus."

"Very true." He thought of his own career, his path to success. Part of it had been tenacity. As if reminding him of that very fact, his phone began to vibrate again. He cursed the timing, then took out his keys and put them into Grace's palm. "Take care of him."

"You know I will." She fished her own keys out of the depths of her bulky coat, then gave them to him. "And take care of my car."

He lingered a while longer, watching Grace and Henry climb onto the sled for the tenth time, then zip down the hill, weaving past the others that crowded the slope. Then he turned and walked away, back to the life he was born to lead.

A life he hated with every ounce of his being.

CHAPTER NINE

BY THE fifteenth trip up the hill, Henry had had enough. Grace gathered up the sled and turned toward the parking lot. "Ready to go back to your grandmother's?"

"Uh-huh." Henry slipped his little mitten-covered hand into Grace's.

She paused a second. Then let her own hand curl around his. The way he walked with her, trusted her, seemed so natural. Which was weird, because if there was one person on this planet who had no intentions of being a motherly type it was her. She'd never considered having children of her own, figuring that she hadn't learned much about parenting from her mostly absent parents, so she had no business thinking she could do a better job. And there had yet to be a man—

Okay, there'd been one. For a short window of time when she'd been eighteen she'd considered becoming Mrs. J.C. Carson, traveling the world for a long time, and eventually settling down somewhere.

But in the years since J.C. she hadn't met anyone who made her want to settle down, put up that white picket fence and a swing on the porch. As she walked along, slowing her pace to match Henry's shorter, boot clad strides, she wondered if maybe she'd missed out on something by steering off the marriage and children path.

Once at J.C.'s car, Grace struggled with the booster seat in the back. Henry climbed in and pointed out where the seatbelt fit and how to click it in. Kid had more mothering skills than she did, for goodness' sake. A clear sign she shouldn't be fooling with thoughts of being a mother herself. She stowed the sled in back, then drove a good five miles under the speed limit all the way over to J.C.'s mother's house.

She hesitated in the drive. The last time she'd been here she'd seen J.C. with another girl. His father's words had still been ringing in her ears. *"He doesn't want someone like you. If you really care about him, then go your own way and let him have his life."*

She couldn't sit in the driveway forever, so she sucked in a breath, got out of the car, and helped Henry out. No one answered the door. Henry danced from foot to foot beside her. "Grace?" He tugged at her sleeve. "I gotta pee."

"Your grandma's not home. Do you think she went to the store?"

Henry shrugged. "She goes to church a lot."

"Oh." Well, that could mean that J.C.'s mom would be back in five minutes—or an hour. Grace had no idea. In the meantime, Henry was wriggling and squirming, and the temperature outside was dropping. "Let's go to my grandmother's house. It's just around the corner. And I'll call your uncle and tell him where you are. Okay?"

When Grace arrived at her grandmother's house with Henry in tow she thought Mary might just explode with joy. "Oh, what a precious little boy! Come here, come here, let's get you some hot chocolate and cookies and—"

"Gram," Grace interrupted, laughing. Leave it to her grandmother to start with dessert. "He needs to pee. Then you can stuff him full again."

Henry slipped his hand into Grace's. Oh, no. She knew what that meant. He wanted her to take him to the bathroom. She looked down at him. Surely he knew what to do and how to do it? "Uh…here's the bathroom," Grace said, leading him to the small room off the main hallway. Thankfully, Henry went inside the room and shut the door. She waited outside, just to be sure he didn't, like, fall in or something.

The doorbell rang, and through the oval of glass Grace saw J.C.'s face. Relief flooded her and she pulled the door open. "You got my message?"

"Yep. Thanks for stepping in and taking care of him. I didn't expect my mother would go out. Again."

Something in the way J.C. said that told Grace a lot more lurked under the surface. More worry, more stress, more secrets. She waited for him to tell her, to open up, even though she knew it was a fruitless wait.

J.C. proved to be the same man as always. The one who kept up the walls around his personal life and kept his emotions tucked in tight. She'd thought on the hill today she'd seen the J.C. she remembered, but she'd been wrong. It made her wonder how well she had ever really known him if he kept so much of himself hidden. He'd rarely opened up about his family life, something she hadn't noticed until after they were over and she'd realized she'd been doing all the talking over the years. Was it because J.C. didn't have anything to say or share? Or didn't he trust her enough to tell her about his feelings, his fears?

Or did he think she would judge him if he did? The glimpses she'd had of his life had painted a sad picture.

J.C. striving for his father's approval as a child and falling short time and time again. John Carson had had few kind words for anyone, most of all his family.

"So tell me the truth. Did you put the pedal to the metal with my car?" She gave him a grin.

"Of course not," J.C. said, then a smile flashed across his face. "I waited until I was on the outskirts of town."

She laughed. "Glad to hear you aren't completely a button-down guy."

Instead of responding, J.C. turned away and rapped on the bathroom door. "Henry, you ready?"

The little boy emerged from the bathroom, soapy hands dripping on the carpet. J.C. laughed, then took him back to finish hand washing. When he was done, Henry pointed down the hall toward the kitchen. "She's gonna make me cookies and hot chalk."

J.C. chuckled. "Hot chocolate, you mean?"

"Mommy called it hot chalk. Cuz the stuff on top is white."

"Oh, yeah. It is." J.C.'s face tightened. He cast a glance at Grace, and she sent him a smile of sympathy.

These little moments, the ones when the loss of Henry's parents returned, almost broke Grace's heart. She barely knew the boy, but she knew how much J.C. had loved his effervescent sister. The absence of her in their lives had to be an intolerable blow.

It also reminded her of the article she wanted to write. Handled correctly, Henry's story could touch a lot of hearts.

"My grandma makes the best hot chalk in the world, Henry," Grace said. "If you hurry into the kitchen, I bet she'll let you help her."

"Okay!" He dashed down the hall and rounded the corner.

Grace heard Mary exclaim, and knew Henry would be in good, if overindulgent hands for the next few minutes. J.C. started to follow, but Grace put a hand on his arm. "Wait a second. I wanted to ask you for a favor."

"What kind of favor?" he asked.

She took a deep breath. "I wanted to profile you and your nephew for my article. I think it adds a human piece to what would otherwise be just an ordinary—"

"No."

"You didn't even hear me out."

"Doesn't matter. I don't want my family and my personal life splattered all over some magazine."

Just like that. Without even letting her finish. "Is that what you think I'd do? Create some invasive harsh piece that takes advantage of you?"

He studied her for a long moment. "No. I don't."

"Then trust me and let me interview you two. Or, better yet, just let me spend time with the two of you and write up an article from that. Nothing formal, nothing stuffy. Just an uncle and his nephew taking in the Christmas magic."

"You want to use my family's tragedy to advance your career?"

She swallowed hard against the truth. "It will also help you get the kind of publicity you want for the festival."

"I have TV crews and reporters are all over the place here, plus the pieces you're writing and the social media you've been implementing. There'll be plenty of PR."

"Yes, but it'll be the kind of articles that talk about the reindeer and the swimming swans." She gave him a smile, but he didn't return the gesture. "Not the kind that touches people's hearts and makes them seek out Beckett's Run because..." She thought of the ice skaters she'd seen earlier today at the park. The Winslows, making a slow circle of the pond, holding hands, laughing with each other. Harriet had had one arm linked with Bert's, her free hand resting on top. She had kept glancing up at him with adoration. Contentment. "Because it's a place for second chances."

"Is that what you're here for, Grace?"

She drew herself up. "We're not talking about me. We're talking about you and Henry."

He shook his head. "Still the same Grace. Avoiding the personal subjects."

"My job is to focus on the other stories that are here, not on myself." She paused, then let out a sigh. How could she be mad at him for not opening up when she did the same thing? "Okay, you're right. I am here for a second chance. My career…well, it hasn't been going so well lately, and I really need a story that will help find my groove again. For me, this isn't just about promoting Beckett's Run, J.C. It's about what I'll be doing after I leave here. And how, hopefully, I'll be able to carve out a new niche. Something that has more depth than just another piece about another hotel in another country."

He considered her for a long moment. "Fine. I'll help you find your story. One that *doesn't* focus on my nephew. I'm sure we can find another heartwarming happily-ever-after for you to use. Deal?"

It wasn't what she wanted, but maybe she could do the same with another story. She could see the protectiveness for his family in his eyes, and couldn't argue with that. "Okay." He turned to go, but she put a hand on his arm. "It's probably not my place to ask, and I wouldn't say a thing if we weren't friends—"

"Friends? Is that what we are?"

"We always have been, haven't we?"

"I'd say we want way past friends a long time ago."

The words, low, dark, sent a rush of heat through her veins. A slideshow of images of her and J.C. in his bedroom one hot summer night while his parents were away at some company event in the city. The window open, a soft breeze drifting over Grace's bare skin as J.C. made his way from the top of her head to the bottom of her feet, kissing, touching, loving every inch of her. And then, when he'd entered her, the stars had exploded in her head and she had thought in that moment that she knew what perfection felt like.

"But in the end we came back to being friends," she said. Because she wanted to believe that. Wanted to believe that hot summer night could be forgotten and they could turn back the clock.

Even if it had never gone that far from her memory, and standing here, in close quarters with J.C., it was all she could do not to think about being in his bed. His arms. His life.

God, she missed him. In a hundred ways that went beyond a bedroom. But J.C. wanted everything she didn't—corporate life, putting down roots, working nine to five—and that meant they could never be together. Hadn't his father made that clear to her? J.C. would never love a vagabond like her. Yet a part of her heard Henry's laughter in the kitchen and Gram's soft murmurs of encouragement and she wondered if roots were such a bad thing after all.

"Anyway, as a friend," she said, pushing the words forward before her thoughts brimmed to the surface, "I wanted to say I know this has to be a hard time for you, with Henry and everything, after the loss of your sister. And…" She took his hand in hers. It felt so familiar, so right. "I'm sorry."

"Thanks."

"Your sister was an amazing person. A force to be reckoned with." She grinned.

"That she was. She'll be missed. More than I can say."

Sorrow filled his eyes again, and Grace wished she could take the pain away. She wished she and J.C. could go back to those lazy summer afternoons by the creek when the biggest worry they had was being home in time for supper. When they'd while away an entire afternoon, doing nothing but catching minnows and eating crackers and listening to the frogs calling to each other.

"I heard what you said about your mom. Is she okay?"

"She's fine. She's just had a hard time after the loss of my sister and sometimes she just…unplugs. It's getting better but it's going to take time." He let out a long breath. "Anyway, it's nothing you need to worry about. I can handle it."

"And run a business from afar. And watch over Henry. And plan a major event for the town. You're super, J.C., but you're not Superman."

He chuckled. "Lately, I'm not so sure I'm either."

"I know you, J.C. You tend to take everything on your shoulders. It's okay to let your mom do more. To expect more out of the people around you. To ask for help, or, heck, admit you can't do it all."

He shook his head. "That's not going to happen."

"I think—"

His features hardened. "Grace, you don't know my life. You don't even really know me anymore. So don't tell me what to do." Then he headed down the hall and into the kitchen.

She stood in the hall for a long time. He was right. She didn't know this grown-up, serious J.C., this billionaire who had become the town hero. Maybe she had never really known the J.C. by the creek, either. And she needed to remember that every time she let the memory of one summer night cloud her thinking.

Two days later, J.C. had to admit Grace knew her stuff. The publicity machine was in full swing, and she had the social media thing down to a tee. She'd covered the snowflake-decorating contest with a quirky, fun story that had gotten picked up by the wire services. That brought more interest in the Santa lookalike contest, and the attendance numbers for other festival events promised to rise. Every hotel in the tri-county area was booked for Christmas Eve with out-of-towners.

They'd had hundreds of visitors from the surrounding area, which had beefed up tourism dollars and created an actual traffic jam in downtown Beckett's Run for the first time that anyone could remember.

The town was abuzz with anticipation for the big event on Christmas Eve, and the out of town media had stepped up their coverage. He'd seen several pieces on the Boston news channels, and even something on the Rhode Island stations. He'd had a call from the *Today* show, and an email from another morning show producer.

Grace had done it all with barely a phone call to him, leaving him free to work. He'd finished the merger in record time, which had taken the stress out of his C.O.O.'s voice.

J.C. knew he should be grateful. It was why he'd asked Grace to be part of the team, after all. And he was—

Sort of.

But he had to admit he had missed seeing her and talking to her. After the disagreement at her grandmother's house Grace had told him she needed to do some work and left him and Henry alone with her grandmother to enjoy the hot chocolate. In the days since she'd kept her distance.

All the while the kisses they'd shared kept springing to the surface, a determined memory demanding he reckon with the implications.

He still found her attractive. He still wondered about her. And he still wanted her. Even though he knew nothing had changed between them—she was still the girl who would rather run than tackle the tough issues, and he was still the guy who would stay and stick it out—he still wanted to kiss her again. And more.

Instead he watched the magic building around him— the sets going up, the events being organized, the decorations being hung—and cursed the workload that kept him busy most of the day. He wanted to get his hands dirty and get right in there, rather than run back and forth to Boston to sit in on yet another meeting. J.C. let out a sigh and dialed the office, turning away from the view before him so he could concentrate.

"I can't believe you pulled that merger off, J.C.," said his C.O.O. when he answered. "In record time, no less. I know everyone's happy to have the holiday off."

"You still heading to Cancún with the wife and kids?"

Charles sighed. "Nah, I'm putting that on hold. My wife's so mad, I'm sure the only thing I'm getting for Christmas is a lump of coal and the cold shoulder."

"You should go," J.C. said. He knew Charles had been planning this vacation for months. It was supposed to be a second honeymoon of sorts for the couple. "I've got this under control."

"J.C., you have enough on your plate. You need someone here in the city to—"

"The company won't fall apart if we both are out of the office at the same time."

"It'll be hurt by our combined absence, and you know it. The last time we were both gone—"

"You worry too much. It'll be fine. Go on your trip." Charles started to interrupt and J.C. cut him off. "That's an order. Life's too short to spend it in an office."

"Is that the same J.C. talking? The one who works more hours than the entire company combined?"

"Hey, it's Christmas. Take this as a gift and run with it."

"Okay, okay. You just made my wife happy, J.C." Charles chuckled, then sobered. "But when we get back in the office—"

"The work will be there." And it would. As it had been the week before, and the ones before that, and all the years since J.C. had taken over his father's company and made it bigger and better than his father could have ever dreamed. But in the process he had become the very thing he'd never wanted to be—a corporate, suit-wearing workaholic who barely had time for his family. His time in Beckett's Run was coming to an end, and J.C. knew as well as he knew the sun would rise that once he went back to Boston he'd be working dawn to dusk, and barely, if ever, see Henry. He thought of the merger he'd just completed—one that would combine his company with another similar in size, giving J.C. an even larger empire to command.

It was what he had worked hard to achieve, but a part of him wondered why. He'd started off filling his father's shoes out of necessity, then growing the company to ensure futures for those who worked for him, and then, at some point, he had found the business becoming a wayward animal that needed constant tending. One he wasn't so sure he wanted to tend anymore.

Life's too short to spend it in an office. His own words, yet he hadn't taken that advice either. He couldn't call the few weeks he'd been in Beckett's Run a break from the office. Given the way his phone remained tethered to his hand and ear, he hadn't really stepped out of the office at all—merely relocated it.

He thought of the day he'd gone sledding with Grace and Henry. That had been fun—real, honest-to-goodness fun. He wanted more days like that. More days when the office was a distant memory. When he thought about music, or enjoyed the bright sun, or played hooky in the middle of the day. But walking away, or selling, meant hurting those who worked for him, and those who depended upon him, and he couldn't do that.

Grace's words came back to him. *"I bet there's a rocker in you still."*

Maybe, but he hadn't picked up a guitar in so long he wasn't so sure he could remember "Smoke on the Water," never mind anything more complicated. He hadn't even brought his guitar to Beckett's Run—and it used to be the one thing permanently attached to him. He'd told Grace dreams like that weren't practical.

That was the word his father had used over and over again. *"Be practical, J.C. Where would you go with a career in music? Nowhere but the unemployment line."*

Maybe so, but would he be happier? Or would he be just as dissatisfied with his days, and wondering if there was more to life than just existing?

He hung up the phone and leaned against a tree as a winter storm started kicking up around him. He watched the snow fall for a long, long time. He remembered the bright laughter of Henry, followed by the teasing voice of Grace.

And when he did he realized what he wanted.

CHAPTER TEN

THE park buzzed with activity. Grace had her pen and pad of paper ready, and had brought along a tape recorder, too, to capture as many comments as she could. Beside her, people were getting ready for the Beckett's Run Winter Festival Snowman Shuffle, one of the last kick-off events scheduled before the big day-long party on Christmas Eve. Two dozen competitors were lined up by piles of snow, ready for some serious snowman building.

She knew she should be focusing on the competition, and on her job, but she found herself looking for J.C. Beside her, Henry danced with excitement. "Can I go watch?"

"Sure." She followed along with Henry, to stand beside the competitors. J.C. was across the park, talking to the construction crew as they assembled a few last-minute items. Christmas Eve was tomorrow, and anticipation rang in the air.

She had yet to get her story. J.C. had introduced her to several Beckett's Run residents with heartwarming tales, but none of them had her mind whirring like Henry's. Thus far she had honored J.C.'s wishes and not probed when it came to his nephew, but her gut told her the real story was right beside her. She needed to talk to Henry some more, and find the angle that would work the best. She watched him gazing at the snowmen with longing, and decided an activity would be the easiest way to get Henry to talk.

"Hey, let's build our own snowman," she said to Henry. "Want to?"

"I'm a good snowman-maker," Henry said. "Uncle Jace says so. He helped me make one 'fore, when the snow was up to here." He put a hand against his chest. "It was a big snowman."

"I bet."

Every time she learned something else about J.C. it surprised her. He was the kind of guy who built snowmen with his nephew and told him stories at night and tucked him into bed. Yes, he worked an insane amount of hours—she had yet to see him without that phone of his, tending to company issues around the clock—but he made time for the littlest person in his life. That didn't jive with the unemotional man she kept seeing in him.

Had she misjudged J.C. all these years?

Instead of thinking about J.C., she bent over and started rolling a small snowball through a pile of snow until it became big enough for a base. Henry joined her, pushing the giant ball around in a circle, then running off to create a second one. Grace let him handle the head of the snowman all by himself, then reached out for the third ball.

"I wanna put it on," Henry said. "P'ease?"

"Uh…okay." Grace bent down and hoisted Henry up. The little boy weighed almost nothing in her arms. He nestled the last snowball on top.

The two of them stood back and admired their handiwork. Henry slipped his little hand into Grace's. She was beginning to get used to the feel of his hand in hers, holding secure and strong, despite his size. "My mommy liked snowmen."

"Did you build one with her?"

Henry nodded. "We named him Earl. Cuz he looked like a king."

Grace laughed. "That sounds like a perfect name." She bent down beside him and started shaping some snow into an arm for the snowman. "What was your mommy like?"

"She was really nice. She liked to watch cartoons with me." As if a plug had been pulled, Henry started talking in a non-stop chatter about his mother and father while they gathered snow and packed it onto the snowman. As their icy creation took shape, so too did the conversation. Henry talked about the way his mother had made macaroni and cheese, and how his father had told him Santa was always watching to make sure Henry was being good, and how angels could fly. It was a conversation that went in ten different directions, then back again, in the way that kids had of circling a point.

Grace heard the longing in Henry's voice and found herself relating. Her parents hadn't died when she'd been little, but they both had been gone so much—after the divorce her father had rarely come by and her mother was always off on one adventure or another—but it was still a loss. Most of her Christmas and summer memories were centered around her grandmother, and her sisters.

And J.C. Carson.

She saw so much of him in this chatty little boy who talked about wanting to be a veterinarian, or maybe a fireman, and definitely a magician when he grew up. She saw J.C. in the way Henry suddenly decided their snowman needed a big head of hair, and she hoisted him up to let him pat snow in a fluffy pile on top. She saw J.C. in the way Henry stood back and put his chin on his hand and assessed the snowman, deciding one arm was too big and one was too little.

And as she and Henry talked about Christmas and Santa and miracles Grace found her story. She could feel it taking shape in her mind, could hear the words she would later put on paper. It wasn't the kind of article she normally wrote, so she wasn't sure how her current editor, Paul, would react. It was the kind of thing she'd tried to write—and failed to do well—during the brief time she'd tried to get a job at *Social Issues*.

Was she up to this challenge? A quiver ran through her.

She glanced over at Henry, at the hope and worry in his little features, and decided she was. He had the kind of story that could touch hearts, and for a writer there was no greater goal to achieve. She could do this. She had to do this.

"Great snowman."

Grace whirled around at the sound of J.C.'s voice. Every time she saw him her heart skipped a beat and she forgot to breathe. He still affected her, even after all these years, and she couldn't decide if that was a curse or a blessing, or a little of both. "Thanks. It's all Henry's doing. He was the brains behind it."

Henry beamed. "I gave him hair, Uncle Jace. Like you!"

J.C. chuckled. "Hair? That's creative as heck, buddy. I'd say that one should take first place."

"Can I go down the snow slide?" Henry asked, pointing across the park. Earlier that day a crew had packed snow onto the kiddie slide and children of all ages—and in thick pairs of snowpants—were riding down and into a cushion of soft snow at the bottom.

"Sure. Just be careful."

But Henry had already run off, and J.C.'s words fell on deaf ears. J.C. laughed. "That kid is so wound up for Christmas. It's all I can do to get him to go to bed at night."

"I remember someone else who used to get excited about Christmas." She gave him a little elbow nudge.

"You couldn't mean me." He grinned. "Okay, maybe when I was little. But Christmas was the one holiday my mother did up huge, and it was impossible not to get excited."

"Gram loves Christmas, too. I think she made the holiday big because she knew us girls were often here instead of with our mom. The few holidays my sisters and I did spend with our mom were always full of last-minute kind of things, like running out to the drug-store on Christmas morning because she forgot to fill the stockings or didn't have any food in the house. She would concoct some grand scheme for a holiday cele-bration, then get distracted by something like knitting us all sweaters, and end up almost missing the holiday altogether." Grace swiped a handful of snow off the back of a park bench and let the flakes tumble to the ground. "I guess that's why I've never been really big on the holiday. Or any holiday."

"Head off the disappointment before it happens?"

"Something like that."

"I can relate," he said quietly. "Is that why you've avoided Beckett's Run the last few years?"

How had this conversation got turned to her so fast? She bristled at the implication that she'd been avoiding the town only because of the holiday connection. Didn't he remember how it had ended? Or had he put his own spin on history, painting her as the villain? "It wasn't just about ditching Christmas, J.C. There was more to it than that and you know it."

"You ran out of here, Grace, and you never looked back."

She whirled around to face him. "Is that what you think happened? That I wasn't hurt by what you did? That I just went on my merry way and forgot everything that happened?"

"Hurt by what I did?" He raised a brow. "You're the one who left, Grace, without a word."

"Because you told me to go." She shook her head. How could he possibly not understand? Not see? Had so many years passed that he had forgotten? Or was he truly that cold? "When I got that call—"

"What call?"

"The one you had your father make. You couldn't even tell me in person, J.C." She shook her head and cursed the tears that sprang to her eyes. She was over this, really over it.

Then why did the pain rear its head again, as fresh as the day it happened?

"Just forget it." She turned to go, but J.C. grabbed her arm and spun her back into him.

"I never told anyone to call you, Grace," he said. "I thought you left because I didn't show up to leave on our trip. I came to your grandmother's house the next day to talk to you and tell you what had happened but you were already gone. *You* were the one who wasn't there for me, so don't go blaming it on some fictional call."

"What do you mean, I wasn't there for you? What happened?"

"Don't you know?"

She shook her head. She'd left town fast and never looked back. She'd stopped in a couple times for day visits with her grandmother, but never stayed long enough to talk to anyone else in Beckett's Run. She'd flitted in and out of this town because every time she turned a corner, something reminded her of what she had lost. And the one topic that had been *verboten* on all her visits had been J.C. Carson, so if something had happened she would have been blind and deaf to it. Had she run too fast?

"Know what?"

"My father had a heart attack that day. I didn't show up because my mother rushed him to the hospital and I had to stay home and watch my sister."

His father had had a heart attack? Remorse filled her chest and she reached for him. Even through the thick fabric of her gloves and his winter coat she could feel the tenseness in him. J.C. had always been like this—an island unto himself—and now was no different. Maybe his withdrawal stemmed from anger at her for letting him down. She wished she could go back in time and redo that afternoon, because no one should go through something like that alone. "I had no idea, J.C. None at all."

"You really didn't know?"

She shook her head. "I would have been there. You know that."

"All these years I thought you left because you didn't want to deal with it."

Was that how he saw her? As a woman who ran at the first moment of need by a friend or loved one? "I would have stayed, J.C. If I had known." She drew in a deep breath and went on. "In fact, I came by your house before I left town. I was going to talk to you about the call. But then I saw you talking to some girl and—"

"Girl?" He paused a second, thinking back. "That was my cousin, Grace. My aunt came in from out of town to help out around the house, and I was talking to my cousin. Because my best friend was gone."

"Your best friend?"

"You."

She'd been his best friend, and he had been hers, all those years ago. That was a bond that would always remain, she realized, no matter how far she went away or how much water went under the J.C./Grace bridge. The friendship was a rock they could each stand on, and that gave her comfort. For a moment she was back there in those bright summer days with J.C. smiling at her, the two of them full of hopes and dreams, talking about everything and nothing. "I'm sorry."

"It's okay, Grace. I understand now. And, really, it was years and years ago."

"I still wish I could do it over." She let out a long breath, watching the air form a frosty cloud in front of her. "Why would your father do that? If he didn't like us being together, fine, tell me that. But why lie and say the message was from you?"

J.C.'s gaze went to Henry, who was twenty feet away, laughing with the other children as they took turns sliding down the slide. Around them, the activity of the Winter Festival hummed, people working like bees in a hive to ready everything for the next night. "He thought you distracted me."

"Me? From what?"

"From my 'destiny.'" J.C. put air quotes around the last word. "To run the company and take care of the family. He saw me getting off track when I ran off with you and did all those crazy things we did, and he kept trying to rein me back in. But I didn't want to do that. Then he heard about our plan to run off, and I guess that was the last straw. I never thought he'd go that far." J.C. let out a curse and shook his head. "I'm sorry, Grace."

"It's not your fault. You didn't even know." She reached for his arm again, and this time felt an easing in the tension in him. He turned to her, his gaze seeking forgiveness and a way back to that bridge between them. "I should have known you wouldn't do that. I should have trusted you."

It was a conversation they should have had a long time ago. One they might have had that day if she hadn't misinterpreted the entire situation. But she'd been acting on hurt, and running had been easier than dealing. Wasn't it always? She'd become her mother, in many ways, dashing away at the first sign of conflict.

But just the thought of staying put, of taking that kind of risk, made her throat close. She took risks in her job—ziplining, bungee-jumping, water-skiing—but not in her emotions.

"Maybe you would have hung around for a couple days, but then you would have gotten that itch to run and you would have hit the road," he said, honesty in his eyes. "It's what you do, Grace. Even when someone needs you."

Hurt tinted the color of his words. All these years she had thought she was the one who had been betrayed and let down, never knowing that he had felt the same way. Her leaving at such a critical time in his life must have seemed like a slap in the face. "I would have stayed a while, yes. And once everything was taken care of, and your father was better, we could have gone on our trip.

Pursued those dreams. Both of us wanted to leave this town, remember?"

"That was a foolish dream. And it was a good thing it never happened."

"What do you mean, a good thing? You wanted to leave as much as me. You ended up still here and working in an office all day. That's the opposite of what you always said you wanted."

"It didn't matter what I wanted, Grace. Don't you understand that? My family needed me and I had to be there. My father was sick for years. I started college, and worked after school and on breaks with him, learning the business from the inside out, trying to keep it afloat so my family could pay the bills and the people who worked for him could pay theirs. People depended on me, Grace. I couldn't just up and leave for some pipedream."

The words hit her like a slap. "That 'pipedream' used to be important to you."

"So was taking care of my family." It had started snowing, and a light dusting of flakes coated J.C.'s hair, his shoulders. "The day after I graduated from college my father died. I stepped into his shoes. And I never left them."

"But…why? You never wanted that life. You never wanted to be tied to that company. To him." The relationship between father and son had been acrimonious at best. Even if J.C. had rarely talked about it, that much Grace had been able to discern from the few times she'd seen them together, and the way his father had looked at her, like mud sullying his son.

"Because people were depending on me. People who needed that paycheck every two weeks. Which meant they needed a Carson to be there every day. Over the years, the company has gotten huge, and now it's like a runaway train that requires me to constantly be on board."

He sounded stressed, overwhelmed. Not at all like the J.C. she used to know. "So sell the company, move on. Live your own life."

"It's not that simple, Grace. I can't just shed it like a winter coat."

"Of course you can. Why do you have to stay and make it bigger and badder? What are you trying to prove?"

He scowled. "I'm not trying to prove anything."

"Well, you did prove one thing. That you're afraid to take that leap into the unknown. To just pick up and go and leave everything behind." She leaned in closer to him. "Is it because you're afraid, J.C.? Afraid of being on your own? Afraid of failing?"

"Says the expert at never getting tied down. You're the one who's afraid, Grace. Not me."

"I've climbed mountains and stood on the edge of volcanoes, J.C. I'm not scared of anything."

He closed the gap between them and put a finger under her chin. "You are terrified of staying in one place. You are terrified of settling down. And, most of all, you are terrified of giving away your heart."

She shook her head. "I already did that. With you. A long time ago. But we'd never work out, would we? You're still going to want to stay here and I'm still going to want to go."

"What is so wrong with staying here?"

She looked around the park. Happy laughter flowed from the people like water out of a spigot. Christmas music piped in from a hidden sound system carried on the air. There was a spirit of hope, of family, of wonder everywhere around her.

"I've learned that nothing lasts, J.C. Especially the things you depend on most."

Then she turned and left, clutching her notepad to her chest. It was her ticket out of this town, and she refused to let it go.

Lights blinked, ornaments gleamed. J.C. came home from working on the festival to find the tree decorated and his mother and Henry standing before it, admiring their work. Henry was beaming, and J.C.'s mother looked tired but happy for the first time in a long time.

"Uncle Jace! We gots the tree up! And the socks! And presents!" Henry grabbed J.C.'s hand and dragged him around the living room, pointing out all the activity of the past afternoon.

"It looks great," J.C. said, raising his gaze to his mother's. "Really great."

"Thank you."

The two words were about a lot more than a compliment, and when his mother reached for his hand and gave it a squeeze J.C. knew it was going to be okay. They'd all been on a long and painful road, but at last they were finally heading into the sun.

"Henry and I are going to make some sugar cookies after dinner," his mother went on. "Want to help?"

"Maybe later. I have a dinner invitation."

His mother arched a brow. "With Grace?"

"Grace's grandmother. She wanted to thank me for having her driveway plowed. Whether Grace will be there or not..." He shrugged. "Who knows?"

"Did you guys have a fight?"

"We talked about some things we should have talked about a long time ago."

The conversation still stewed in his mind. All these years he and Grace had gone without speaking because of a misunderstanding. No, not a misunderstanding—

An interference.

Resentment rose in J.C.'s chest. After all he had done for his father, for the family company. John couldn't have let his son have that one relationship? Of course if J.C. had stayed with Grace he would have left Beckett's Run and never worked at the company. Never been there for his mother, and now Henry.

"All these years I thought Grace left without me," he said. "Turns out there was a lot more to the story than that."

"Henry?" J.C.'s mother said, bending to talk to her grandson. "Would you like to watch a Santa movie until dinner's ready?"

"The one with the reindeer? I love that one!" Henry clambered onto the sofa and waited while the movie was loaded and started.

J.C.'s mother gestured toward the kitchen. The two of them went into the other room, and while his mother started boiling some water and mixing up a quick spaghetti sauce J.C. took a seat at the table. "I knew about the call," his mother said.

"You did?"

She nodded. "When he was in the hospital, your father told me what he did. By then Grace was already gone and you were working at the company, and I didn't say anything because…" She let out a long breath. "I didn't want to rock the boat. It was always easier to keep the peace than to go to war."

That had been his mother's job. To soothe the waters, mend the broken fences. He wondered if she'd been happy married to his father, or if she'd stayed because of the kids. It was too late now to ask such questions, and a part of J.C. didn't want to know the answers anyway. His mother had been widowed for several years now, and before the death of her daughter she'd been active, living a new life. Traveling, taking music lessons, indulging her only grandchild. She had worked part-time at the library, even though J.C. provided her with a generous monthly stipend.

She'd kept the peace, and for that J.C. was grateful. His mother had been the true rock of this family, even if she didn't realize it. He crossed to her and gave her a warm hug. "It's okay, Mom. I understand why you did it."

She turned in his arms. Tears brimmed in her eyes. "Do you?"

He nodded. "Your number one concern was your children, and that's what a mom is supposed to worry about. Dad was hard on us—"

"Especially on you."

"But I guess in the end he wanted the same thing. The best for us." J.C. let out a long breath and stepped back, leaning his weight on the counter. "I wouldn't agree with his methods, but I see the why now. And after working his job for several years, I can also understand why he was so short with people at the end of the day. Being the boss is tougher than it looks."

"In some ways, I wish you'd never taken over the company," his mother said. "You should have gone on that trip with Grace, J.C. I should have encouraged you. Packed your bags for you. Instead, you stayed and you helped the family and put everything you wanted on hold."

"If I'd really wanted to go, Mom, I would have," he said, realizing that truth for the first time. He could have easily walked out the door all those years ago and headed off with Grace. Or, heck, left at any time. But he never had. "I think a part of me wanted to work at the company. To prove I could do it."

"To prove you were better than what he said."

J.C. shrugged, as if that didn't matter, but he knew there was a part of him that had always wanted his father to acknowledge the job his son had done. To stop criticizing and compliment. Just once.

"He was proud of you. He just never said it."

J.C. dropped into a chair again. "He had plenty to say, Mom. None of it was ever good."

His mother put down the spoon in her hand and came over to the table. She sat down across from J.C. and covered his hand with her own. "Your father was a hard man. Never one to admit a weakness or, even worse, show one. But he loved you, even if he didn't always tell you the way he should. And even if he made a few mistakes in trying to protect you. He said all that to Grace because he thought he was protecting you."

"Protecting me?"

"He didn't want to see you get hurt. Not by Grace, but by the world. He knew that if you went out there into the great unknown with your guitar you'd risk rejection and disappointment. And he didn't want that for you. He wanted you to go into the family business because he knew you'd do well there."

"And he could control the outcome."

"Maybe. I think it was more that he wanted to be there, as much as possible, to guide you and watch over you. He worried about you and your sister's futures. He wanted to be sure you'd be okay long after he was gone."

She squeezed his fingers and a soft smile stole across her face. "And you, my dear son, are more than okay. You have far surpassed anything your father or I ever dreamed of for you."

"Financially, yes. But personally..." He let out a breath and looked away. "I gave up a lot when I took over that company."

"You have a chance now to have what you missed," his mother said. "Don't let your life keep passing you by."

"Someone has to run the company, Mom. And take care of Henry. And—"

"And you can ask for help. Henry will be fine here with me. And the company will be fine if you step down and let someone else take over. You've made your money, J.C., you've proved your point."

"It's not that easy, Mom, to walk away."

"Yes, it is." Her words held firm conviction. "What are you afraid of?"

"I'm not afraid of anything."

Hadn't he had the same conversation with Grace today? She'd accused him of being afraid and he'd turned it around on her. Maybe he'd been wrong all these years. Maybe Grace wasn't the fleeing jackrabbit.

Maybe he was.

His mother patted his hand, then got to her feet and reached for the spoon again. "Then go after what you want, J.C. It's Christmas. A time for miracles and hope. And new beginnings."

She pressed a kiss to his temple, as if he was six all over again and about to head off for his first day of school.

And maybe, J.C. thought as he got to his feet and reached for his coat, he was. He was heading off for his first day of something new—something he had denied himself for a long, long time. Maybe his mother was right and it was time for him to do the very things the detour into the company had put on hold—

Risk rejection and disappointment.

CHAPTER ELEVEN

THE doorbell rang just before dinner. Grace finished fixing her hair, then headed for the stairs. Gram hadn't mentioned anything about company for dinner, and as far as Grace knew her sisters weren't due to arrive until tomorrow, Christmas Eve.

There had been two dinners with her mother this past week. The meals had been strained and short—both times, Grace had used her work on the festival as an excuse to leave early. It wasn't that she didn't love her mother, it was that she was tired of believing in change that would never come.

Her mother kept talking about how she'd settled down now. Was planning on buying a house, planting a garden. Grace wanted to believe her mother was different, but past history was a cruel teacher and Grace had learned her lessons well, as had her sisters.

Soon she'd be back at work and would be able to put off seeing her family for another year. She thought of the article she had written after building the snowman with Henry. She had yet to send the email, because for the first time in forever she was nervous. Not just about whether the editor would love the piece as much as she did, but because somewhere in the writing her view of the article had shifted.

It was no longer about saving her career. It was about sharing a piece of her heart. She had opened up a vein to her soul on the page, and what mattered now was that people connected with that. Whether she got a job at *Social Issues*—or, heck, anywhere after this—was no longer important.

The doorbell rang again. Gram called out, "Coming! Just a second."

Grace paused at the top of the stairs while Gram opened the door, and as if conjured up by Grace's thoughts Lydia stepped into the house.

Followed by Greg McKinnon.

Grace stared at her parents—divorced, remarried, divorced again—standing together with wide smiles on their faces. "Hi, Grace. Hi, Mary," Lydia said. "And… well, surprise."

Surprise didn't even begin to describe it. Grace couldn't find a word to say.

Her grandmother stepped forward first, drawing her son into a hug, then reaching out and giving her former daughter-in-law one, too. "So good to see both of you."

Grace stayed where she was, processing the sight in the foyer. Her parents together again? When had this happened?

Lydia reached for Greg's hand and held it tight. She smiled at Gram. "Thank you for inviting us for dinner."

"You invited them for dinner?" Grace said, descending halfway down the stairs.

Gram nodded. "Your mom said your dad was flying in today, and I thought what better way to start bringing the family together than at dinner tonight?"

"I'm so glad you did, Mom." Greg looked over at Lydia and smiled, then raised his gaze to his daughter.

"I know this is a surprise, honey, but we didn't want to say anything until we were sure."

"Sure? About what?"

He grinned. "Well, your mother and I have been talking over the last few weeks, mostly by phone, a few times in person."

Mom blushed—actually blushed. "Several times in person."

"Anyway," her father went on, "when we realized you girls would all be here in town at the same time, well, we thought we'd make it official and come for Christmas, too."

"Make what official?" Grace said. She had yet to leave her perch on the stairs, as if she was half in the room and half out of it.

"We're back together. For good."

The words seemed to ring in the hall. An excited avalanche of questions and good wishes followed, led by Gram. Grace stayed on the stairs, and wondered how her sisters would take this twist when they arrived tomorrow. Chances were good that Hope, the leader, would take it in stride and be the first one to congratulate everyone. Faith, who had been fathered by another man between the McKinnon marriages, had always held onto a little guilt that she might have been the reason for the marriages' demise, and would be the most reticent, though she'd be her usual warm self around their parents. They'd all congratulate and offer best wishes, and support this new twist, Grace was sure.

But Grace knew better. Her parents were as different as oil and water, and had never been meant to share a roof. This reunion would be lucky to last as long as the wrapping paper on the presents.

She was tired of people not facing the truth. Of thinking some fantasy was going to come about just because they wanted it to. The reality was simple—some people weren't meant to be together and wishing otherwise didn't make it better.

"What's changed?" Grace asked. The conversation came to a halt and all eyes turned to her. "Because, last I checked, the two of you were the same people as always, albeit a little older. And that means you'll get together, honeymoon for a few weeks or a few months, and then, *wham*, end up hating each other again. At least there aren't any little kids to catch in the crossfire this time."

Lydia crossed to her daughter. Behind her, Gram gave Grace a look that asked her to tame her thoughts. But Grace didn't want to gloss over this. She didn't want to put on some happy family holiday event, knowing that as soon as the New Year rolled around the fiction would fade.

"We're older and wiser now, Grace," Lydia said. "We—"

"Don't tell me that, Mom. You haven't changed. You're still everywhere but with us. And Dad's still working a million hours, and waiting for you to come back."

"I'm here now," Lydia said. "With all of you. And so is your father."

"It's a little late for that, don't you think?" Grace hurried down the stairs, grabbed her coat from the hook by the door and pulled open the front door. She stepped out into the cold, even as her mother protested that this time was different.

Grace ignored the words. She'd heard them before.

J.C. found Grace sitting on the porch, bundled in her coat, and watching her breath form puffy clouds in the cold air. The sky held the promise of snow, and the tart crispness of winter. It was going to be a white Christmas, which seemed to add that extra element of magic to the holiday and the Winter Festival. Right now, with Grace sitting there so quiet and sad, the festival was far from his mind. He put the flowers in his hands on the porch and sat down next to Grace.

She gave him a wry grin. "No matter where I go in this town, you pop up like a dandelion."

"It's a small town."

"Not that small."

"True." He gestured toward her. "You look upset."

"My parents are here. And my sisters are on their way." She waved a wide circle. "All one big happy family for the holidays."

"That's good." He caught the arch of her brow. "Isn't it?"

She shrugged. "You know my family. We've never been happy. My parents were separated or fighting more than they were together, and my sisters and I…well, we've never quite gotten along."

"Why?"

Such a simple question, but as Grace considered it she realized the answer was far from easy. Why *hadn't* the three McKinnon girls stayed close? It would have seemed, given the way their mother was always leaving, that they would have banded together more, and stayed that way. There'd been years when they'd been inseparable, but as they'd gotten older the gulf had widened. "I don't know. Sibling rivalry, I guess."

"Want to talk about it?"

"No." She bit her lip. "Yes. But…"

"But what?"

She pivoted to face him. "What are we, J.C.? Friends? More? Old flames?"

He grinned. "How about D.—all of the above?"

"That's not an answer."

"If you don't like the answer, ask a different question."

She let out a gust. "You are a frustrating man."

"Me? I'm easy. Some would even say nice."

"Some?" She arched a brow.

"Well, only a few opinions really matter." He gave her another grin, then sobered. "Come on, Grace. Lean on me for a little bit."

She bit her lip and considered him. The hood of her coat shielded most of her face from the cold, and from his view. "I've always done that. The trouble is, you've never done it with me." An icy breeze ruffled the flowers in their paper wrapper. Cars passed by on the street, tires crunching on the snowy road. Grace let out a long breath. "All the years I've known you, J.C., you've barely opened up about your life or your family. Most of what I know I figured out on my own after seeing you with your parents."

He leaned forward, bracing his elbows on his knees. The cold skated down his back, lifting the back of his jacket. "You don't understand, Grace, how hard it is for me. I didn't grow up in a house where we wore our emotions on our sleeves. In fact, showing any emotion at all…" He let out a gust. "Well, it was a sign of weakness. A strongly discouraged weakness."

"And yet you wanted me to be the one to pour my heart out to you." She raised one shoulder, let it drop. "That's not a friendship, J.C., or, heck, even a relationship."

She was right. He hated it, but she was right. All

these years they'd had a one-sided relationship where he listened and she talked and he never reciprocated. At the time it had seemed easier. If he didn't talk about it, it didn't exist—or, more, it couldn't hurt him. His father's distance, the constant judgment, the ridiculous expectations. Would telling Grace have helped alleviate some of that stress and tension? Made his childhood an easier row to hoe?

He couldn't go on keeping his emotions locked up tight. Where had that gotten him?

The answer came like a punch to the gut.

"I've turned into my father."

Grace didn't say anything. She didn't have to. Her silence was agreement enough.

"I vowed all my life to not be like him, and yet here I am, working at his desk, spending my life in the same office and cutting myself off from the people around me." He let out a curse. The change had come on him so gradually he'd never noticed. The only difference was that he didn't have any children in the mix. Well, he hadn't had any children. But now there was Henry, and as soon as J.C. returned to Boston, to his daily schedule, he knew the job would suck up his time. Henry would be the loser in that equation. "That's not what I wanted."

"You aren't like him, J.C. You're here, in town, with your mom and Henry. You're—"

"Half the time I'm here I'm working. Hell, two-thirds of the time. That's not being with my mother or Henry or you. That's being..." J.C. let out a long breath, and with it, the truth "...him."

"Then stop doing that," Grace said. "If you don't like your life, change it, J.C."

"My mother told me almost the same thing." J.C. shook his head. "That's easier said than done. The company is counting on me. My family is counting on me. Heck, this whole town is counting on me. I can't let those people down."

"You could always do what I do and hop on the next plane out of here."

He grinned. "That's not funny. Okay, maybe it is. I can just see the headlines now if I did that."

A part of him wanted to take Grace up on the offer. Head to Logan Airport, plunk down his credit card and book the first available flight to anywhere. Leave his cell phone behind and just be somewhere no one knew him or wanted anything from him. A good idea in abstract but not in reality. The company would be plunged into chaos if the C.E.O. disappeared, and poor Henry and J.C.'s mother would be left adrift.

"How did you do it?" he asked her.

"Do what? Take off for destinations unknown?" She shrugged. "It's scary, especially when you're traveling solo. That first trip, when I left Beckett's Run, was the most terrifying. I'd never really traveled, and never left the state of Massachusetts. But I knew that if I could handle that, I could handle anything."

"And now? Still ready to hop on the next plane?"

"A part of me always is," she said. "When I stay in one place too long, I get…antsy."

"And are you antsy now?"

"There you go again, turning the conversation into a Grace confessional." She gave him a smile, one that said she wasn't going to answer the question. "We're not talking about me, remember?"

"Old habits die hard," he said with a grin, then he sobered. "You're right, though, about me. I'm sorry for not opening up to you. I should have done that all along. Maybe then we could have avoided what happened that last day, because you would have known that I would never have had my father call you like that."

She interlaced her fingers and wrapped her arms around her knees, drawing her body in tight. "I think a part of me did know that, but I was so hurt I refused to admit it."

"From now on, I swear—" he crossed his heart "—to tell you all my deepest, darkest thoughts."

She laughed. "That could lead down some very dangerous paths."

"Yes, it could." His hand reached for hers. She uncoiled herself and shifted toward him, her eyes wide. When they touched, the familiar electric charge ran through him and desire rushed through his veins. Damn, he wanted her. Not just physically, but in every way. How could he have ever let this woman out of his life?

"Would that be so bad? If we went down those dangerous paths?" he asked.

She held his gaze for a long time, and he wondered if she was thinking of those lazy summer days by the creek, or their long walks through the park, or these last few days, when it seemed like something had been rekindled.

Finally, she released his hand with a sigh, and he realized her thoughts weren't on the same road as his. "I don't know, J.C. I look at my parents and I think anyone would be crazy to get married. They've been on again and off again as often as a light switch. They get married, divorced, date, marry, divorce. Then they realize all the reasons they broke up and they have a huge fight and it's over again." She bit her lip, and sadness washed over her eyes. "My parents couldn't keep it together because they wanted totally different things out of their lives. My father is the worker and my mother is the hum-mingbird, flitting from thing to thing."

Now he saw what she was trying to say. This was a part of why Grace kept pushing him away. "You think we're like that."

"We're exactly like them. I can't repeat that, J.C. I've seen firsthand how that yo-yoing can destroy people. Not just them, but me and my sisters. We never knew which way was up or who would be in the living room when we got up in the morning. My parents loved each other, but that wasn't enough."

"That doesn't mean we'd end up the same way, Grace."

Why wouldn't she trust him? Why wouldn't she take that risk? Every time he thought she'd changed—and he'd thought that a hundred times over the last few days when he'd seen her with Henry and working on the fes-tival—she came right back to this familiar refrain.

"Yeah, we would." Resignation filled her features, and he knew the battle was lost before it even began. "I've known you a long time, J.C., but I only realized today that I've been the one doing all the talking. You kept so much of yourself from me. You keep telling me that I'm the one running, but you are, too, J.C. Running and hiding behind this wall you have up between you and the rest of the world. It's still there, even if you say it isn't anymore. You want me to trust, to take a chance, and yet…you don't do either."

"I do trust you."

"No, you don't." She reached into her coat and pulled out a sheaf of papers. "Remember I told you I wanted to write a story about Henry? And you told me not to?"

"I didn't want you to do that because—" He cut off his words before he said something he'd regret.

"Because you didn't trust me to do it right. To not turn your nephew and your family's loss into some sensationalized piece. That, right there, *that's* the problem. You know me, J.C., and yet you don't trust me. Is that about me? Or you?"

"Grace—"

She pressed the papers into his hand, cutting off his words. "Read that. Please." Then she got to her feet and buttoned her coat around her neck. "And see if I was as self-serving as you thought I was."

"I never said that."

A sad smile flitted across her face. "You never had to." She took a step off the porch.

"Where are you going?"

Her gaze went to the street, then the town beyond, and finally to the horizon. "Anywhere but here."

"Don't go. It's almost Christmas." He reached for her. He could see her pulling back emotionally, and soon, he knew, she'd get on a plane and be a hundred, a thousand miles from him. And he'd have lost her again. "At least stay for the holiday. Beckett's Run is a wonderful place—one of those towns that just sort of wraps around you if you let it, Grace."

She shook her head. "I don't belong in this small town life, J.C. It doesn't matter what day of the year it is."

"How do you know that? You can't find out what you have or what you truly want if you keep leaving, Grace."

But she had already headed down the stairs and off into the gathering storm.

Grace walked for hours, traversing the town that she knew so well she could map it in her sleep. Then she returned to Gram's house—to a quiet, dark home. Everyone had left and Gram had gone to bed early. In typical Gram style she'd left a note and a plate of dinner on the counter for Grace.

Missed you at dinner, but saved you some chicken and dumplings. Get a good night's sleep, Grace, dear. Everything looks better in the morning.
Love,
Gram

Grace took the plate and the note up to her room. She considered her backpack, sitting by the door, packed and ready to go. She could leave tonight and be on an airplane headed to some island somewhere before the sun came up.

Then she thought about what J.C. had said about how she was always running. For the first time in her life the thought of getting on the road again exhausted her. She was tired of being afraid of staying, of taking personal risks.

Tomorrow she would decide. For now she didn't want to deal with any of that. Didn't want to make a decision any more complicated than what pajamas to wear tonight.

But she did make one decision. She set up her laptop, sent out a single email, ate her dinner and then crawled into the bed she had slept in a good portion of her life and fell into a deep, dreamless sleep.

When the morning dawned, the smell of fresh coffee dragged Grace out of bed and down to the kitchen. She didn't check her email first. Coffee before disappointment, she decided.

She had just poured a cup when her oldest sister came into the room, a little sleep-rumpled. Grace reached for a second cup and filled it with hot coffee. Her sister had blue eyes and blonde hair, her features tempered by a wisdom and intelligence that came from being the one they'd all relied upon and turned to when their parents were gone. Or, at least, they used to turn to. The days since either Grace or Faith had done that were long past.

Grace knew she shouldn't be surprised to see Hope—Gram had only mentioned a thousand times that the other McKinnon sisters were coming for the holiday—but she was. Grace loved Hope and Faith, and missed seeing them, but over the years the three of them had drifted apart. They'd gone their own ways, maybe more used to not having connections than building them. Some days she wondered if it was too late to rebuild the closeness they'd had when they were little. Maybe they'd all grown up a little, or rather a lot, and instead of having a relationship where one sister was the substitute mom they could all have more equal footing. Friendship.

"Hey," Hope said, a slight smile on her face. "Where's Gram?"

"Hey, yourself." Grace handed her sister the cup. "Gram's helping out with one of the events today. She went to bed early. I got in late…" She let the words trail off, not wanting to explain everything that had happened in the last few days, or the muddle of emotions running through her.

"I heard you. That board on the porch, remember?" Hope grinned and the shared memory, the common secret, connected them for a moment. "It always did cause you trouble. With J.C. then, too, if I remember right."

J.C. The last person she wanted to think about today. She'd left him with her article, and with a lot of hard questions, and he had yet to contact her. Not so much as a text message. Had she made a mistake?

Instead of dwelling on what couldn't be undone, she

changed the subject. "There's a lot to do to get ready for today. I need to be out the door soon." She paused, the mug warm against her hands and the sight of her sister warm in her heart. It had been a long time, too long, and Grace wondered how she could have let all those months build up. Her sisters used to be her anchor, the two people in the world she knew she could always depend upon. When had she let that go? And why? "It's good to see you, Hope."

"Really?" Hope sat down at the table. "After our last talk…"

Grace waved a hand. The argument no longer mattered. At the time, Grace had blamed Hope for the failure of her own career, which wasn't fair. At all. Grace had been her own undoing, and after last night she began to understand why. She hadn't been pouring her heart into her stories. She'd been running from emotion on the page as surely as she ran from emotion in her own life. Until she'd met Henry and finally opened up.

"It doesn't matter now. It was good for me to come back. To see Gram. To…" Grace let the sentence run off. *Had* it been good to be here? To reopen old doors? Like the ones with J.C.?

Because right now his silence hurt. A lot. She'd started falling for him all over again, and Grace suspected this time the leaving would be ten times harder than when she'd been eighteen.

She forced a smile to her face. "Anyway, how was ranch life?" she asked Hope. "Gram said you were taking pictures for some therapy-type place?"

Hope blushed, and then began to tell Grace about the therapeutic riding facility she'd been working at. When Grace asked if that was all that was making her blush, Hope hesitated. "I thought you had to skedaddle?" she said.

Grace was tired of running. Of not being there for her family, her friends, and most of all for herself. Where had it gotten her? Nowhere but on another plane, to another destination, none of which filled her like these moments in Gram's kitchen.

"Beckett's Run is a wonderful place—one of those towns that just sort of wraps around you if you let it, Grace."

J.C.'s words rang in her head. What did it say about this town that it was the one place she returned to over and over again? The only place that drew her back? Grace dropped into a chair opposite her sister. "I can manage a few minutes."

Hope's gaze met hers and the moment extended between them. One filled with forgiveness, connection, love. And just like that the years melted away and the sisters became sisters again, as if they were little all over again, twin beds pushed together, whispered secrets exchanged long after the light had been turned off.

"The guy that owns the place...Blake...I kind of got involved."

As Hope talked about Blake, and falling in love with the sexy rancher, Grace listened and smiled and—

Envied her sister.

Hope had done it. She'd leapt off that cliff and dove headfirst into the murky waters of love. A world that came without guarantees, or even so much as a promise of happy forever. It was a risk and, looking at the happiness radiating from every pore of her older sister, a risk worth taking.

At the end of the conversation Grace embraced her sister, then told her to bring her camera to the festival.

An idea brewed in Grace's head. One that came with a little risk—

And hopefully a lot of reward.

CHAPTER TWELVE

J.C. STOOD in the park and admired his handiwork. Well, his and about a dozen other people's. The entire park had been converted into a winter wonderland, and people from Beckett's Run and several surrounding towns were walking from section to section, enjoying the steaming hot cocoa, the crisp-fried dough, the ornament-decorating stations. The Winter Festival was a success, and with the last events finishing up tonight he finally felt like he could relax. Breathe. Think.

He had a lot of decisions to make in the coming days. One he needed to make right now, he thought, as his gaze caught on a familiar figure in a dark blue coat standing by the pond. His heart leapt and his pulse raced, and all he could think about was getting to Grace as fast as possible. He wove his way through the crowd, answering the questions that others peppered him with, and accepting thanks from the townspeople, until he finally reached the pond. Ice skaters circled the space, some hand-in-hand, some solo. Grace stood on the sidelines, her arms wrapped around herself.

For a second he watched her, admiring the graceful curve of her neck, the slight smile playing on her lips. Damn, she was a beautiful woman. She teased him and tempted him, and made him think about all the things he had put on hold for so long.

He'd dated women over the years, but none had stuck in his mind or heart like Grace McKinnon. Just the thought of her leaving made a pain rise in his chest. But if she stayed, what could he offer her?

An instant family with Henry, and a husband who worked an insane amount of hours? That would never make Grace happy. She had made it clear she didn't want to be tied down. The best he could do was let her go, and let her find her happiness on the road.

But not quite yet. Not without telling her what he had come here to say and taking one more chance. He had missed that chance all those years ago, and he refused to let it happen again.

He crossed to her. "You came."

She turned to him and a wider smile crossed her lips. "Had to see how it turned out. It looks wonderful. You did an amazing job."

"Thanks. I owe a lot to you. Our attendance is up twentyfold. Maybe even more."

"I didn't do much."

"You did a lot, Grace." And she had. Her publicity efforts had spawned a ton of media interest, and a serious boost in revenue for the town. Business owners had been thanking him all day, gratitude and relief on their faces at the increase in their daily totals. He could only hope the effect lingered, and that people returned for next year's Winter Festival. Beckett's Run would never become a major city or a top destination, which was just fine with J.C. and probably most everyone in town, but it would be nice to see the town get its due share of the tourism pie.

"Did Henry enjoy the parade?"

J.C. chuckled. "He loved it. Sat on my shoulders and watched every single second of it. At the end, Santa gave him a little wave and that just made Henry's day. He's at my mom's right now, helping with some chores, because he wants to be extra good before Santa arrives."

Grace smiled. "He's an adorable kid. I'm glad to see he's enjoying Christmas."

"He deserves it." J.C. let out a long breath and thought of all Henry had been through and the strides his nephew had made in the last few weeks. They weren't out of the woods yet, but it was a start, a good one, and J.C. was glad he had been a part of it. "It's the least I can do."

She put a hand on his arm, let it linger for a second. "You're a good man, J.C."

He scoffed. "I don't know about that. I think I'm working on being a good man."

She shook her head. "You always were a good man. Everything you've done in your life, you've done with the best intentions. You took care of your family, and even this town, because you cared. There's nothing wrong with that."

He wanted to protest, but he saw the earnestness in her face, and for the first time in his life let the compliment fill him with a sense of accomplishment. "Thanks, Grace. That means a lot."

It meant more than he could say. He was still working on that opening up thing.

She shrugged, as if it was no big deal. "Anyway, I better take a walk around the festival. I need to write up a post-publicity piece."

"Wait. I wanted to talk to you about that article on Henry." He reached into his coat and withdrew the typed pages she had given him yesterday. They were a bit wrinkled from his many readings, last night and again this morning. "It was…amazing. Hell, it even brought a tear to my eye. You captured him perfectly, and brought the whole thing full circle with the story about making the snowman."

"Thanks." A blush filled her cheeks.

"I had no idea you could write like this, Grace. I mean, I've read some of your articles—"

"You've read my travel articles?"

He smiled at her. "You don't really think I forgot all about you when we broke up, did you? Of course I read your articles. I'd pick up magazines all the time and look for your name in the bylines. The people in the bookstore must have thought I had some kind of travel bug, given how many I bought. It was my way of making sure you were okay, I guess."

"As long as I'm water-skiing in Florida, or shopping the outdoor markets in Indonesia, I must be fine?" She smiled, clearly touched that he'd done that.

"Something like that." He reached up and brushed a lock of hair off her forehead. "I never forgot you. I tried, but you're a pretty unforgettable woman, Grace McKinnon."

"J.C.—"

"Don't." He put a finger on her lips. "Don't tell me not to say this. Don't tell me you don't want to hear it. And don't leave before I finish." He lowered his hand and decided if he didn't tell her this now he may never get another chance. All week he'd wanted to take this risk, to open his heart to her. If she still left at the end, at least he would know he had told her how he felt— how he'd always felt. Even before he spoke, he could see the familiar fear in her eyes, the urge to bolt. "I have never forgotten you. Never found anyone who is like you. And I don't want you to leave. Not today, not tomorrow, not ever."

"We can't—"

"Don't." He grinned to soften the admonishment. "I woke up this morning and realized, after reading your article, that there's only one thing I want to give Henry, and myself, for Christmas this year." He exhaled the breath in his chest, and with it the words that would change his future. Put him on the path he had foregone many years ago. "I'm selling the company and I'm staying here."

Before his first cup of coffee J.C. had called the owner of the company that was expecting to merge with Carson Investments and offered the other man the opportunity to play out the merger in reverse, with the other company bringing Carson Investments under its wing. They'd hashed out the details, and a tentative offer was in place. It was done, and though this decision would have ripples throughout Carson Investments, J.C. knew it was the right move. A long-overdue move, at that.

Grace blinked. "You're...what?"

"Moving back to Beckett's Run. For good. I've made my money. I've proved my point. Now I want a life. And I want one right here, where my family is, where my heart is." He grabbed her hands with his own and held tight. "I know you want to leave, Grace. I see it in the fear in your eyes and the way you're only half here. But I'm asking you to reconsider. Stay here with me in Beckett's Run and let's take that journey we planned all those years ago."

"Back then we were going to ride off into the sunset and go where the wind took us."

"The wind brought us both back here at the same time this year. I don't think that's a coincidence. I think it's a sign that we have a second chance, and we'd be fools not to take it."

She searched his face. Doubt and questions knotted her brows, drew lines in her forehead. "What are you saying, J.C.?"

"I'm saying I love you and I always have. I want you to stay, Grace. I want you to take a chance."

She was already backing up, already letting go. "I can't, J.C. My career takes me all over the world and—"

"That's an excuse. You can still be a travel writer. You can still go to Bali and Cancún and all those places. But when you are done come home to me, to Beckett's Run."

"What if it doesn't work out? What if we do this with the best intentions and we end up breaking up? What if we have children caught in that? Kids like Henry, who don't need any more hurt in their lives?"

"Are you saying that because you don't love me, too, or because you're afraid of turning out like your parents?"

Beside them, the skaters continued in their endless circle, skates whispering softly on the ice. A light dusting of snow began to fall, the sun catching each flake and making it sparkle.

"I'm exactly like my mother, J.C.," Grace said. "I can't settle down. I can't stay. Even the thought of doing that scares me to death. So I know that even if I say yes to you right now, I'm going to get antsy and I'm going to leave again someday."

"Why did you write that article about Henry?" he asked.

She shook her head at the change in topic. "What?"

"Just tell me. Why did you write that article?"

"Because I knew his story would touch people's hearts."

"I've read what you write, Grace, and it's nothing like that. I mean, your articles are good, but they aren't the kind that tackle deeper issues like this one did. So why this story? Why now?"

She let out a breath, and though she didn't come any closer she didn't move any farther away, either. "When I was in Russia a few years ago I met this little girl. It was early winter, and it was so cold. She didn't even have a coat, and yet she was standing on the street corner, trying to sell newspapers to feed her family. I bought a paper, took her to a store to buy a coat and fed her every day that I was there. She moved me, J.C., and I decided I wanted to write a story that would make people notice little girls like that. And do something about it. So I wrote that story and I sent it off to my college professor, who's the editor at *Social Issues,* the kind of magazine that covers those things. He rejected it."

"Why? You're a fabulous writer."

"I have what it takes to write about the best hotel for your honeymoon, or some hidden getaway in Costa Rica, but when it comes to the stories that matter I'm not good enough. The editor said it was because I didn't put my heart into it. I tried to do it with this article on Henry, because this time it mattered to me. More than whether my career would be there tomorrow. But I don't know if I accomplished that." She raised her gaze to his and tears shimmered in her eyes. "That's why my articles don't move people, and that's why I don't stay, J.C. If I did, I'd have to put my heart into this place, and my heart's been broken so many times that I just can't do that anymore."

Grace McKinnon, abandoned and left dozens and

dozens of times as a little girl. The youngest of the McKinnons, and the one most affected by their mother's frequent departures. He'd always thought of her as the strong one, the one who seemed to have it together the best. When really that had all been a front. "You're not afraid of counting on other people, Grace," he said gently. "You're afraid of other people counting on you."

She opened her mouth to argue, shut it again.

"If you don't hang around, if you don't put down roots, no one is going to expect you to step up to the plate. To be the leader." He shook his head and gave her a smile. Grace, a woman so good at reading and writing about other people, couldn't see the stories in herself. "What you don't understand is that you have been the leader forever. You were the one who took all the chances, who encouraged me to step outside the boundaries. You gave me the childhood and teen years I never would have had, and you taught me to take risks."

"All I did was get in a lot of trouble, J.C. I didn't do anything else."

"You took off on an around-the-world trip by yourself at eighteen. Who does that? You're the bravest woman I know, Grace, and yet you don't see it. I wish you would." He reached up and cupped her jaw, and met the eyes that he loved so much. "I wish you'd take a chance on loving me. Because I've taken that chance on you." Then he pressed a tender, easy kiss to her mouth, praying it wouldn't be their last kiss. "Come back to the festival tonight. There's something I want you to see. I'll be in the gazebo around seven."

"J.C., I don't think I'm staying for the rest of the festival. I need to get back on the road and on to my next assignment."

He let his hand drop away. "You already have your

next destination, Grace. It offers everything you've ever been looking for. And then some."

If Grace had been hoping for peace, she didn't get it. She parked in front of Gram's house, walked inside the door, and was swamped by a flurry of hugs and good wishes from her sisters. Hope and Faith sandwiched her between them, giggling and talking as if no time at all had passed since the three had seen each other, while Gram stood to the side with two men Grace didn't recognize. Their parents were also there, also standing to the side, chatting with the men.

The whole family. Together for the holiday. Grace wanted to run back out the door, but she couldn't—not with everyone between her and the outside. She thought of the backpack upstairs, packed, ready to go.

Then she thought of J.C.'s words. He loved her.

Loved her.

How long had she waited to hear that? And now that she had all she wanted to do was run in the opposite direction. Because her heart was beating too loud and too fast to think about anything else.

"It's about time you got home," Hope said. "We've been waiting for *hours*."

Grace pushed a smile to her face. "Sorry. Got tied up at the Winter Festival."

"We were afraid you were going to run out of here before Christmas. It wouldn't be a proper holiday without you, too, Grace." Faith gave her sister a quick, tight hug.

Grace returned the warm embrace and vowed that, no matter what, she'd be sure to keep in better contact with her sisters. For too long they'd been flung all over the world—England, Canada, Australia—and it was time the McKinnon sisters banded together and stayed that way.

"And now that we have so much news to share, you have to stay."

"News? What news?"

"We're getting married!" Hope and Faith exclaimed at the same time.

They dragged over the two men, introducing them as Blake and Marcus, their new fiancés. Hope and Faith talked over each other, rushing to tell all about the rancher who had stolen Hope's heart and the Earl who had Faith blushing.

"That's wonderful," Grace said, drawing each of her sisters into a hug. That feeling of envy raised itself in her chest again.

J.C. had asked her to stay, to start a life with him here in Beckett's Run. She could be celebrating with her sisters if only she'd take a chance. She felt torn in two, her heart and mind warring for two different courses of action.

"That's all really wonderful," she repeated to Hope and Faith, then turned to Blake and Marcus. Given the way they were beaming at her sisters, she had no doubt the two men were in love, and determined to give Hope and Faith happy futures. She was happy for her sisters, who deserved that happy ending.

What about you? her mind whispered.

Grace tried to breathe, but her throat suddenly felt tight, her chest seemed as if a twenty-pound weight sat on her heart, and she turned away, grabbing the newel post like a lifeline. "I have a…a deadline to meet. Let me just run upstairs and get this emailed out, and I'll be back to catch up with all of you soon. Okay?"

"Sure, sure," Faith said. "We'll be here for a few days. We have lots of time to catch up."

Grace hurried up the stairs. She dashed into her room, shut the door and lay down on the bed. Her heart raced, her breath whistled in and out of her chest, and her mind raced. What *was* all this? She was never this discombobulated or scattered.

A knock sounded on her door. Grace scrambled to her feet, reaching for her backpack to feign the work she'd used as an excuse, but Gram entered the room first.

"You doing okay, kiddo?"

"I'm fine. Just…busy." The closed laptop and empty desk belied the statement.

"Too busy to spend time with your sisters?"

"I will…later."

Gram crossed the room and came to sit on the corner of the bed. "Honey, I know it's hard for you. In fact, I think sometimes it's hardest on you out of all them. Hope was the oldest and she kind of took charge. That gave her something to do, something to focus on when your mom would leave. Faith was in the middle and, oh, such a vocal girl about everything. But you, my sweet, dear, Grace, you were the youngest. The one who got forgotten sometimes."

Grace shook her head, but her eyes burned all the same. "It was okay."

"No, it wasn't. And I think you put up walls and distance because that keeps you from getting hurt. Going on trips, staying too busy for family get-togethers, and jetting off at the last minute are all walls, just a different kind." Gram cupped Grace's face in soft hands. "Sometimes you just have to take a chance, Grace, and love other people. And stay still long enough for them to love you."

"I just… It's hard for me." She bit her lip and willed the tears to stop. They didn't listen. "I understand why Mom did it. I think she was scared. Scared of falling in love, scared of being hurt."

Gram considered that for a moment. Her wise light blue eyes were filled with kindness and understanding when they met Grace's. "I think you're right. But I also think this time your mom and dad are going to make it work. I've listened to them and watched them together. After losing each other the second time, I think they finally changed and grew up. Realized what's important and how much they love each other. How much work it takes to keep that together."

"And how scary it is to fall in love with someone?" There. That was what had her throat tight and her breath caught. The fear of falling in love. With J.C.

"Exactly," Gram said. "Did you know your grandfather had to ask me four times to marry him?"

"Four times? You never told me that."

"Oh, he was a stubborn one. Good thing, too, because he turned out to be more stubborn than me. I didn't want to settle down and get married, which in my day was a crime against nature and society." She chuckled. "I was afraid that if I got married it would make me give up my freedom. I'm like you. I want to make my own rules, decide my own fate. It took me a while to realize that loving someone, and being loved back, gives you more freedom than anything else in this world."

"How's that?"

A soft smile stole across Gram's face, and Grace could see her reaching back in her memory for the man who had been with her most of her life. Even now, with him dead and buried for many years, her love was evident and strong. "Their love becomes the gust of wind beneath you. It helps you soar higher. Your grandfather encouraged me in every crazy idea I ever had. And, you know, your father did that with your mother, too. He wanted her to find herself, and it took some time but she did. Now look at them."

They *had* looked happy this week, Grace realized. Happier than she could ever remember seeing them. She thought of her sisters, and how each of them seemed to have become more themselves with the men they loved by their sides. If she took that chance, would she find the same thing?

She glanced at the backpack. Battered and worn by all her travel, all her destinations. She'd been all over the world, and in the end she'd come right back to the beginning. A sign, J.C. had called it. A sign of what?

"Anyway, I've said my piece." Mary gave her granddaughter a hug, then drew back. "It's Christmas Eve, and after dinner we're all heading over to the festival. One big happy family. Exactly what you asked Santa to bring you every Christmas, my sweet granddaughter. You finally have what you wanted. Now, come enjoy it."

The Monday Morning Carp Club sent J.C. a wave as he passed them on his way through the park. The dance was in full swing at the pole barn set up outside of Santa's Village, and the rest of the park was filled with visitors trying out the enticing sweets and rides. He glanced at the Mistletoe Wishes ride as he passed, and felt a pang.

Grace.

She'd taken off out of the park after their conversation earlier today, and hadn't returned. He had tried calling her a couple times, but his calls went straight to voicemail. Because she was on a plane somewhere? Or because she didn't want to talk to him? Either way, the answer wasn't one he wanted.

He saw his mother and Henry coming toward him, Henry's little legs pumping fast to keep up with his grandmother's longer strides. Both of them were smiling and walking hand in hand. Henry released his grandmother's hand and dashed toward J.C., who bent down, put out his arms and scooped up his nephew. J.C. knew as long as he lived he'd never get tired of doing that, or get tired of feeling Henry snuggle into him with a joyous hug.

"Uncle Jace!" Henry said, drawing back. "We saw Santa! And he says he's coming to my house tonight! He says I've been a good boy!"

J.C. ruffled Henry's hair. "You have indeed. I think Santa's going to bring you lots of gifts."

"Spoil him rotten, you mean," his mother added, and shot her son a teasing smile. "Hopefully Santa didn't make any more toy store runs today."

"Maybe just one." J.C. grinned, then released Henry. He reached for the item in his mother's hands. "Thanks for bringing this. I'm surprised you found it."

"That attic is full of all kinds of forgotten things," she said. "I also got out some of your toys from when you were a kid. Henry prefers those to the ones his mom had, as any boy would. I should have done that a long time ago." She sighed. "I guess I was just trying to bring her back."

J.C.'s chest grew tight. He missed his sister, too, and the loss seemed to sting more as the holiday neared. "She's in every smile Henry gives us, Mom. And in every laugh. She's right there, right with us. All the time."

His mother came to stand beside him and watched her

grandson talking to some other children. A proud smile stole across her face. "You're right. I raised a pretty smart son, didn't I?"

His gaze scanned the park. But nowhere did he see a familiar blonde ponytail. "I guess so. Right now, I don't feel so smart."

His mother patted his arm. "She'll be here. I know she will. I'm going to go grab Henry and get a seat. I'll talk to you later, son. Good luck." She pressed a kiss to his cheek, then headed toward the gazebo.

J.C. stood a while longer in the cold, while snow dusted his head and shoulders. People milled about him, but he paid them no mind. Across the way he saw committee volunteers Walter and Sandra walking arm in arm, and he envied them their moment of romance.

His phone dinged with a reminder of the hour. Seven o'clock. And Grace wasn't here.

J.C. let out a breath, then headed toward the gazebo and the tent erected over it, put in place earlier today to create an indoor space in the outdoors, a shelter against the cold. His shoes crunched on the snow, and to his ears the sound seemed to echo. He peeled back the clear paneled entrance to the tent, headed down the aisle past the assembled townspeople, sending a wave to the Beckett's Run Book Club as well as his mother and Henry, then climbed up the stairs and took a seat in the center of the gazebo.

"I'd like to welcome you all to the Beckett's Run Winter Festival," he said into the microphone. "I hope you've all had a great time."

A collective cheer went up from the crowd, followed by a burst of applause.

"Thank you. But I couldn't have done this without the help of many fabulous volunteers. And now—"

The panel peeled back again. A blonde stepped into the tent.

Hope McKinnon, followed by a brunette. Faith McKinnon. Two men joined the women, then Grace's parents, and finally her grandmother, Mary. The panel slid shut again. The hope in J.C.'s chest died. He cleared his throat and swallowed hard against the disappointment. He couldn't do this.

"Anyway, I know you all were expecting a performance tonight," he said, his hand lighting on the case beside him, "but—"

The panel opened again. Grace stepped into the tent and raised her gaze to his. A moment passed, then a smile winged across her face and hope took flight in J.C.'s chest again.

"But I'll delay it no longer," he said.

He undid the clips on the side of the case and withdrew the wooden acoustic guitar inside. It wasn't the top-of-the-line electric guitar that he'd taken with him to college, which sat in a closet gathering dust in his Boston home, but rather the first guitar he'd ever owned—a gift from Santa when J.C. was ten years old. The same guitar he'd used to bring on those trips to the creek. In the quiet of lazy summer days he used to played songs for Grace while the crickets chirped and the birds added a melody.

Now Grace walked down the aisle and took a seat in the front row, between her grandmother and his mother. Henry climbed down off his seat and into Grace's lap, leaning back against her chest. She hesitated only a second, then wrapped an arm around him and leaned down to whisper in his ear. He grinned, then nodded and settled in to listen.

J.C. strummed a note, paused as a moment of panic flooded him, then let out a breath, closed his eyes and started playing again. The haunting melody from an old song came back to him with each note, and before long he had added his voice, too. It had been years since he'd played in front of any kind of audience—and never had he played in front of anyone in Beckett's Run, except for Grace—but the song came easily after a while, and as people began to move along to the beat he relaxed and let the music carry him forward.

When he was done, the audience erupted into applause. J.C. got to his feet, did a comical bow, then introduced the next musical act before leaving the stage.

When he got down the stairs, Henry started toward him, but J.C.'s mom held her grandson back and told him to wait a bit. Grace's family got to their feet and greeted him, and though he returned the friendly words, and gave hugs to Hope, Faith, Mary and Lydia, his attention stayed on Grace.

"I think we need to make some room," Hope said to Faith. "For Grace's happy ending."

The two sisters laughed, then stepped aside, leaving a direct path from J.C. to Grace. As he closed the distance between them everyone else in the room dropped away. He saw, heard, noticed nothing but the way her eyes lit up as he approached. Her hair was down tonight, dancing around her shoulders and tempting him to come closer, to touch the silk tresses. His fingers flexed at his side. Damn, he wanted her.

"Thanks for coming," he said. As far as lame opening lines went, that one had to be at the top of the list. For only the second time in his life he was nervous around Grace. As if he was sixteen again and about to ask her on a date.

"I recognize that guitar," she said. "In fact, I remember it very well."

He grinned. "I hoped you would."

"And the song. You used to sing that to me."

He nodded, and in her face he saw she was think-ing of those summer days, too. Back when they had thought there was nothing outside the little world they had carved out for themselves. "I never sang it for any-one else before today."

"Really? Why?"

"You're not the only one afraid of risk," he said with a smile. "You know the real reason I didn't go on that trip with you? I was afraid of failing. Of taking that risk and proving my father right. That I'd never make it with my music and I'd end up pumping gas at a gas station for a living. So I kept my music just between you and me. But I don't want to do that anymore. I'm not look-ing to make a career out of this, or to have a hit record, or anything other than just enjoy playing. I don't care about being the next big thing; all I care about is show-ing you that I'm serious."

"Serious about what?"

"About taking more risks from here on out." He leaned the guitar against a nearby chair, then took a step forward, closer to her. She stayed where she was, which J.C. took as a good sign. A very good sign. "If you want to leave Beckett's Run, Grace, and travel the world, I'm ready to go with you. To take that chance on the unknown. I don't want to lose you, and if that means leaving here, then so be it."

"I don't want you to do that," she said, sending a glance in Henry's direction. The little boy clung tight to his grandmother's hand, watching the exchange. Grace sent him a smile, and Henry returned the gesture. "I don't want you to do that at all."

J.C. sighed. His heart sank. He'd expected her to say

anything but that. "Okay. Well, thanks for coming to the show, and thanks for helping with the festival." He turned to go, but before he could take a single step she put a hand on his arm and stopped him.

"I don't want you to do that because I want you to stay right here and raise Henry and help this town get back on its feet, and…" she took a deep breath and let it out with a smile "…be with me."

"Be with you?"

She nodded, and now the smile widened, lit up her eyes. "I'm not going anywhere. I'm staying right here in Beckett's Run, with you and Henry and my grandmother. I love you, too, J.C., and I always have. I never told you before, and I should have, a long time ago, because you are my first and only love, J.C. Carson, and I can't imagine being with anyone else."

"Oh, Grace, I love you, too." Joy threatened to explode inside him. He met her gaze with his own. In her eyes he saw the reflection of his own heart. She did love him, and the thought filled him with a happiness he had never known before. "I've realized in the last few days that it doesn't matter how much money I make, or how much I achieve, if I'm alone at the end of the day. I want to begin and end my day the same way every time. With my best friend."

She grinned. "Is that what we are, J.C.? Best friends?"

He closed the gap between them and placed his hands on her waist. "I think we're best friends. And a lot more."

"A *hell* of a lot more," she emphasized, then leaned in and kissed him. A light, easy kiss, that lasted barely a second before she drew back. "I don't want to run anymore. I don't want another stamp in my passport. I want to stay right here with you and build a home."

"Doesn't that scare you?"

She laughed. "It terrifies me. But I'm the girl who traveled the world by myself. I'm pretty sure I can handle a white picket fence and a dog in the yard."

He chuckled. "I think I can handle that, too. Though I have to admit my mowing skills are pretty much nonexistent."

"Then we'll get goats." She laughed again, a light, merry sound, then leaned into him again. "And you know I don't care if the lawn is perfect or the dinners get burned or the paint starts to peel. That kind of thing has never mattered to me."

"Me either." He drew her even closer to him, then gave her a long, sweet kiss. Behind him, he heard the excited, happy chatter of their families. He drew back. "But what about traveling the world? Writing?"

"Turns out you were right about that article on Henry. The editor at *Social Issues* loved it. He wants me to write more pieces like that. Now you've said it's okay, he's going to run it in the next issue, and I asked my sister Hope to take some pictures of Henry to go with it."

J.C. had seen Hope's work. He couldn't think of a better accompaniment to Grace's powerful words. "That's awesome. Maybe someone else who has lost a loved one will read it and find comfort."

She nodded. "You know, when I wrote that story, I thought I was writing it for other people. So they would read it and remember the true meaning of Christmas."

"And what is that?"

"That family trumps any present in the world. It's the one thing Santa can't bring, a store can't sell, but you can create yourself." She glanced over at her family, all standing on the sidelines, watching her with smiles on their faces. "When I wrote that article, I realized what was different about this one, as opposed to the one about the girl in Russia. I put my heart into it, J.C., because I opened my heart. To Henry. To you. To this town. And when I thought about leaving again…" She let out a long breath, "I just couldn't go. I love it here. It's the same as it was when I was a little girl, and probably will be when I'm an old lady, and that's what I love the most about Beckett's Run. You can depend on the book club to meet on Tuesdays and the diner to serve chicken pot pie. I'll probably have to travel some to research articles, but in the end…" she grabbed his hand, giving it a slight squeeze "…I'll always come home to Beckett's Run."

"To me."

She nodded. "To us."

God, he loved hearing those words. He didn't think he'd ever tire of hearing Grace saying she wanted to be with him. "Does this mean you want to take that journey with me? Because I have the riskiest trip of all planned."

She cocked her head. "What's riskier than skydiving in Malta and scuba diving in Australia?"

"Marrying me." He gave her a grin, and took her other hand. For a man who usually prepped and planned, this was one time when J.C. hadn't done either. Another step outside the lines for him. He had a feeling he'd be doing a lot more of that in the months and years to come, and it felt good. Liberating. "I know I'm not doing this right, and I don't even have a ring—"

"You're doing this exactly right, J.C.," she said softly. "You're asking me to marry you in front of everyone who loves us."

Someone cleared their throat behind him, and he heard the soft murmur of anticipation from the crowd assembled in the tent. "Not to mention in front of the whole town."

She laughed. "I couldn't think of a better audience." Then she surged into his arms and a smile broke across her face. "Yes, J.C. Yes, I'll marry you."

And as J.C. leaned in to kiss his soon-to-be-wife, the woman he had loved since that first bite of chicken pot pie, he heard Walter behind him mutter, "It's about time," while the rest of Grace's family and J.C.'s family sent up a collective cheer and loud congratulations.

He kissed Grace for a long, long time, and even when the kiss ended he held on to her. She leaned against his chest, and J.C. thought how right and perfect that felt, and always had.

The book club ladies came over to offer their best wishes. "I'm so glad you're staying in Beckett's Run," Pauline Brimmer said to Grace. "You can be a part of the book club every week now."

Grace put up a hand. "Oh, I don't know about—"

Pauline cut her off with a dismissing wave. "Don't forget, we're reading *Little Women*. I think you're going to love the ending. The last scene with Jo and Mr. Laurence is just so…" she put a hand to her chest and sighed "…romantic."

Grace looked up at J.C., at the man she had loved for as long as she could remember, and shook her head. "I don't need to read it. I already know how the story ends. They got married, settled in the perfect small town, and, most of all, they lived happily ever after."

Then she took J.C.'s hand and headed out into the falling snow as Christmas Eve came to an end and a new beginning began.

* * * * *

COMING NEXT MONTH from Harlequin® Romance
AVAILABLE JANUARY 2, 2013

#4357 THE HEIR'S PROPOSAL
Raye Morgan
Tori was the butler's daughter, Marc the heir. He's still out of her league, but can being unexpectedly thrown together lead to second chances?

#4358 THE SOLDIER'S SWEETHEART
The Larkville Legacy
Soraya Lane
When Nate left Sarah, he broke her heart. But now he's back in Larkville. After all that's happened, there's still that spark between them....

#4359 THE BILLIONAIRE'S FAIR LADY
Barbara Wallace
When Manhattan heiress Roxy enlists the help of hotshot lawyer Mike, suddenly it's not just her future at stake—it's her heart....

#4360 A BRIDE FOR THE MAVERICK MILLIONAIRE
Journey Through the Outback
Marion Lennox
From relaxing cruise to thrilling Outback adventure, Finn takes Rachel on a wild ride! But Rachel's still reeling from her painful past....

#4361 SHIPWRECKED WITH MR. WRONG
Nikki Logan
Rob and Honor couldn't be more opposite! But marooned in paradise, Honor discovers that even playboys have their good points....

#4362 WHEN CHOCOLATE IS NOT ENOUGH...
Nina Harrington
For Daisy and Flynn their chocolate business deal equals their ultimate dream. But soon they're tempted by something even sweeter....

HRCNM1212

REQUEST YOUR FREE BOOKS!
2 FREE NOVELS PLUS 2 FREE GIFTS!

Harlequin® Romance

From the Heart, For the Heart

YES! Please send me 2 FREE Harlequin® Romance novels and my 2 FREE gifts (gifts are worth about $10). After receiving them, if I don't wish to receive any more books, I can return the shipping statement marked "cancel". If I don't cancel, I will receive 6 brand-new novels every month and be billed just $4.09 per book in the U.S. or $4.49 per book in Canada. That's a savings of at least 14% off the cover price! It's quite a bargain! Shipping and handling is just 50¢ per book in the U.S. and 75¢ per book in Canada.* I understand that accepting the 2 free books and gifts places me under no obligation to buy anything. I can always return a shipment and cancel at any time. Even if I never buy another book, the two free books and gifts are mine to keep forever.

116/316 HDN FESE

Name	(PLEASE PRINT)	

Address		Apt. #

City	State/Prov.	Zip/Postal Code

Signature (if under 18, a parent or guardian must sign)

Mail to the Reader Service:
IN U.S.A.: P.O. Box 1867, Buffalo, NY 14240-1867
IN CANADA: P.O. Box 609, Fort Erie, Ontario L2A 5X3

Not valid for current subscribers to Harlequin Romance books.

**Are you a subscriber to Harlequin Romance books
and want to receive the larger-print edition?
Call 1-800-873-8635 or visit www.ReaderService.com.**

* Terms and prices subject to change without notice. Prices do not include applicable taxes. Sales tax applicable in N.Y. Canadian residents will be charged applicable taxes. Offer not valid in Quebec. This offer is limited to one order per household. All orders subject to credit approval. Credit or debit balances in a customer's account(s) may be offset by any other outstanding balance owed by or to the customer. Please allow 4 to 6 weeks for delivery. Offer available while quantities last.

Your Privacy—The Reader Service is committed to protecting your privacy. Our Privacy Policy is available online at www.ReaderService.com or upon request from the Reader Service.

We make a portion of our mailing list available to reputable third parties that offer products we believe may interest you. If you prefer that we not exchange your name with third parties, or if you wish to clarify or modify your communication preferences, please visit us at www.ReaderService.com/consumerschoice or write to us at Reader Service Preference Service, P.O. Box 9062, Buffalo, NY 14269. Include your complete name and address.

HR11B

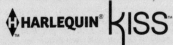

* * *

"LET's go now to the tent and make love...." Emir's mind stilled when he tasted her lips; the pleasure he had forgone he now remembered. Except this was different, for he tasted not a woman, but Amy. He liked the still of her breath as his mouth shocked her, liked the fight for control beneath his hands, for her mouth was still but her body was succumbing. He felt her pause momentarily, and then she gave in to him. But there was something unexpected, an emotion he had never tasted in a woman before—all the anger she had held in check was delivered to him in her response. A savage kiss met him now, a different kiss than one he was used to. The gentle lovemaking he had intended, the tender seduction he had pictured, changed as she kissed him back.

"Please..." The word spilled from her lips. It sounded like begging. "Take me back...."

Except he wanted her now. His hands were at the buttons of her robe, pulling it down over her shoulders, their kisses frantic, their want building.

She grappled with his robe, felt the leather that held his sword and the power of the man who was about to make love to her. She was kissing a king and it terrified her, but still it was delicious, still it inflamed as his words attempted to soothe.

"The people will come to accept…" he said, kissing her neck, moving down to her exposed skin so that she ached for his mouth to soothe there, ached to give in to his mastery, but her mind struggled to fathom his words.

"The people…?"

"When I take you as my bride."

"Bride!" He might as well have pushed her into the water. She felt the plunge into confusion and struggled to come up for air, felt the horror as history repeated—for it was happening again.

"Emir, no…"

"Yes." He must know she was overwhelmed by his offer, but he didn't seem to recognize that she was dying in his arms as his mouth moved back to take her again, to calm her. But as she spoke he froze.

"I can't have children…."

* * *

Can Amy stop at one night only with the enigmatic emir?
Especially when this ruler drives a hard bargain—
one that's nonnegotiable…?

Pick up
BEHOLDEN TO THE THRONE
by Carol Marinelli on December 18, 2012,
from Harlequin® Presents®.